THEATRE SYMPOSIUM
A PUBLICATION OF THE SOUTHEASTERN THEATRE CONFERENCE

Theatre and Film

Volume 19

Published by the

Southeastern Theatre Conference and

The University of Alabama Press

THEATRE SYMPOSIUM is published annually by the Southeastern Theatre Conference, Inc. (SETC), and by The University of Alabama Press. SETC nonstudent members receive the journal as a part of their membership under rules determined by SETC. For information on membership write to SETC, P.O. Box 9868, Greensboro, NC 27429-0868. All other inquiries regarding subscriptions, circulation, purchase of individual copies, and requests to reprint materials should be addressed to The University of Alabama Press, Box 870380, Tuscaloosa, AL 35487-0380.

THEATRE SYMPOSIUM publishes works of scholarship resulting from a single-topic meeting held on a southeastern university campus each spring. A call for papers to be presented at that meeting is widely publicized each autumn for the following spring. Authors are encouraged to send unsolicited manuscripts directly to the editor. Information about the next symposium is available from the incoming editor, E. Bert Wallace, Campbell University, 108 Fine Arts Building, Buies Creek, NC 27506, wallacebe@campbell.edu.

THEATRE SYMPOSIUM
A PUBLICATION OF THE SOUTHEASTERN THEATRE CONFERENCE

Volume 19

Contents

2011

Introduction

THE PAPERS IN this volume were selected from work presented at the April 2010 SETC Theatre Symposium. In the call for papers, scholars were invited to examine the mutual influence of theatre and film through consideration of shared history, present practices, and ongoing connections. They were challenged to contemplate the following questions: Can we enrich our understanding of theatre through more extensive consideration of the closely related art of film? In what ways do film and theatre borrow from each other? Are theatre scholars and practitioners overly defensive in asserting the unique aspects of live theatrical performance due to the greater popularity of film? Given the exact reproducibility of film, along with transferability to video, DVD, Internet, and so on, movies are widely available. Beyond ease of access, do theatre and film really make different demands on audiences? Or, is the job of spectating much the same for both art forms?

Interested participants gathered at Agnes Scott College for a weekend of papers and discussion about these and related questions. The papers offered many different perspectives on the relationship of film—broadly construed by presenters to include video and digital media—to live theatrical performance. Theatre Symposium keynote speaker Bruce McConachie made the case that similar cognitive abilities are involved in viewing both theatre and film. As he remarked in his address, "Most of the mental operations that *Homo sapiens* deploy to make sense of live performances are also used to understand filmic ones." He further argued that "[w]hile there are important historical differences among live and mediated modes of communication, they share a common evolutionary and cognitive foundation." A version of McConachie's keynote talk, entitled

"Theatre and Film in Evolutionary Perspective," is included in this volume. It is joined by eight other papers chosen from the twenty-four presented during the symposium.

In her essay "Melodramatic Borrowings: Life, Stage, Screen," Erin Bone Steele examines the recycling of nineteenth-century British murder melodramas as low-budget films in the 1930s. The next two papers both involve theatre artists with an interest in incorporating film or mediated images into their stage work. In "Robert Edmond Jones: Theatre and Motion Pictures, Bridging Reality and Dreams," Anthony Hostetter and Elisabeth Hostetter explore the influential American scenic designer's vision for using film as a backdrop to convey characters' inner lives and communicate on the level of symbols and unconscious thoughts. Advances in technology since the early 1950s when Jones imagined a "theater of the future" have made the inclusion of film and video images in stage productions much more prevalent in recent years. Director Frank Castorf is one theatre artist whose work regularly features mediated material, both prerecorded images and live video feed, as a prominent element in his theatrical productions. Steve Earnest considers the aims of Castorf's "dual aesthetic of theatre and film" in his essay "Frank Castorf at the Volksbühne am Rosa Luxembourg Platz: Alienation Techniques and the Use of Mediated Material on the Live Stage."

Two of the papers grapple with the anxiety generated as traditional stage practice engages with new media technologies and as a home video industry threatens to supplant a nation's live theatre. In "The London Theatre Goes Digital: Divergent Responses to the New Media," Leslie A. Wade explores the ways the British stage has embraced digital media and discusses how differing attitudes to the new technology on view in two recent theatre productions reflect a larger cultural debate. Becky Becker examines how a burgeoning film and video industry in Nigeria threatens to destroy a once vibrant theatre culture in her paper "Nollywood: Film and Home Video, or the Death of Nigerian Theatre."

Another set of writers explore various ways films and videos can incorporate theatre, theatricality, and even the performativity traditionally ascribed to "live" theatre. Nathan Stith in "The Performative Nature of Filmed Reproductions of Live Performance" looks at Coco Fusco and Guillermo Gómez-Peña's performance piece *Two Amerindians Visit the West* and the resulting documentary, *The Couple in the Cage,* along with Sacha Baron Cohen's mockumentary *Borat.* Stith highlights the ways audiences for the mediatized reproductions bring different awareness and knowledge to screenings than that possessed by the audience members for the original live performances. In "Play-within-a-Play or Theatre-in-Film? Ingmar Bergman's *Through a Glass Darkly,*" Lawrence

D. Smith observes interesting filmic borrowings of theatre elements in the work of Bergman and his contemporaries. Nenad Jovanovic also looks at a use of theatrical form and content within film in "Montage and Theatricality as Sources of Estrangement: A Tendency in Contemporary Brechtian Cinema."

As usual, the intimacy of the gathering allowed Theatre Symposium attendees to hear every paper and engage in conversation throughout the weekend. I would like to acknowledge all the presenters, who contributed to the success of the event. In addition to those whose work is included in this volume, they are Gayle Austin, Jane Barnette, Evan Bridenstine, James Buglewicz, Kathryn T. Farley, Nestor Bravo Goldsmith, Joshua Jeffries, Susan Kattwinkel, J. Patrick McNamara, Wes D. Pearce, Sarah Powers, Robin Roberts, Laura Sava, E. Bert Wallace, Graham Wolfe, and Christine Woodworth.

We held this Theatre Symposium on the beautiful campus of Agnes Scott College in Decatur, Georgia. I am especially grateful to David Thompson, Annie Louise Harrison Waterman Professor of Theatre at Agnes Scott College, for his generous assistance with local arrangements. I am also thankful for the work of the editorial board in carefully reviewing the papers submitted for publication. Philip G. Hill, founding editor of *Theatre Symposium,* and Scott Phillips, chair of the Theatre Symposium steering committee, have been terrific resources throughout my association with the publication. Thanks also to Betsey Baun and the staff of the SETC central office, Daniel Waterman and the staff at The University of Alabama Press, and E. Bert Wallace, associate editor for this volume, who is taking on the job of editor for the next two volumes. Finally, thanks to the Department of Theatre and Dance at Wake Forest University and my esteemed colleagues for various kinds of support, assistance, and encouragement.

J. K. CURRY
WAKE FOREST UNIVERSITY

Melodramatic Borrowings

Life, Stage, Screen

Erin Bone Steele

All audiences engage in various decoding processes when making sense of any work of art.[1] Our previous training allows us to recognize genres, and to navigate new works through our knowledge of conventions and our willing suspension of disbelief. "Melodrama" and "melodramatic" are imprecise terms that are usually used to refer either to emotional content or to a historical genre; people think they know melodrama and its characteristics well, and often dismiss it as overly simplistic or lacking in literary merit, or expand the term to encompass so much that it becomes useless to a scholar. Nineteenth-century melodramas, however, functioned in significant and complex ways, capitalizing on audiences' expectations to provide entertainment that also reinforced cultural ideals of the lower and middle classes, adjusting dramatic messages as those ideals shifted. Subgenres naturally developed, including nautical, imperial, gothic, romantic, exotic, and true-crime plays. And although melodramas in the United States and in England share many characteristics, there are also differences that naturally arise from each distinct nation's unique anxieties and social issues.

During the nineteenth century, the working poor in England attended the melodrama theatre in droves even when the "legitimate" theatres were rebuilding their houses to segregate their patrons by class. In 1811, when architect Benjamin Dean Wyatt was hired to rebuild the venerable Drury Lane Theatre, one of London's two licensed playhouses, one of his stated goals was to protect the "more rational and respectable" patrons from having to pass through crowds of "disreputable" people.[2] Illegitimate or unlicensed companies producing melodrama, however, catered to that excluded crowd and built playhouses in working-class neighborhoods, particularly in the East End. These theatres offered entertainments that generally furthered moral lessons and often presented issues about temperance, crime, working conditions, poverty, imperialism, nationalism, slavery, and women's rights, usually employing sensational special effects to heighten the audience's enjoyment. As Michael Hays and Anastasia Nikolopoulou write in their introduction to *Melodrama: The Cultural Emergence of a Genre,* "The claim for a linkage between the melodrama and the political and social conditions of the world in which it emerged seems quite unproblematic."[3] This is not to suggest that there was not also a complicated process of interpretation and expectation informing what an audience might or might not take away from viewing a particular production, but melodrama does have much to tell us about interpretation and representation designed for a particular popular audience.

British melodrama authors in the mid-nineteenth century engaged in an interesting process of source choice and narrative reworking. Quickly adaptable source material became a major consideration when the economic situation of London theatre created a harsh environment for playwrights after 1820.[4] Minor theatres offered their writers a fixed price for a play; the playwright had no hope of receiving benefit performances, copyright protection, or what might now be called royalties on future productions. Playwright Douglas Jerrold had a relatively good position earning five pounds a week as house dramatist for the Surrey Theatre in the 1830s, but Jerrold earned a grand total of only sixty pounds for one of the century's most famous melodramas, *Black Ey'd Susan.* Beyond literary works and folk tales, theatres and playwrights found useful subject matter in popular crime events, loosely translated from newspapers to the stage. "The consequences of the low market value of drama after about 1820 or 1830 were obvious," says melodrama expert Michael Booth. "Authors either had to turn out great quantities of material very quickly or abandon the drama entirely. . . . The only way an author could keep up the monetary pace at the low rates prevailing was feverishly to adapt French plays, work to a few stereotyped situations and characters, steal from popular novels, dramatize newspaper reports of crime, rewrite his own old plays, and borrow liberally from his fellow dramatists."[5] Most of these hardworking commercial writers churned out melodramas that, not surprisingly, did not hold up well as literary texts and were not preserved in their own day, let alone in modern scholarly circles enamored with the development of Realism.[6] However, as Thomas Postlewait reminds us, "Melodramatic and realistic dramas developed during the same period. . . . We make a categorical and historical mistake when we attempt to fix their identities." Melodrama is not just an immature or inferior form of theatre: "It has its own achieved form, fully developed and immensely popular since the end of the eighteenth century. Of course it has gone through changes, as do all art forms."[7]

A similar set of circumstances seems to surround the British film industry in the 1930s and subsequent discussions of film works created during the early twentieth century. The rapidly produced low-budget "quota quickie" films made in Great Britain during the 1930s, as studios rushed to satisfy the Cinematograph Films Act, are often held in contempt by film scholars. As Lawrence Napper writes in one book review, "The results have long been held in contempt by critics and scholars as both unwatchable in themselves, and detrimental to the reputation of British cinema overall—an ironic consequence of legislation whose main purpose was to protect and enhance British filmmaking."[8] Although all studios had to bring a certain level of technical investment and expertise to the filmmaking process, popular entertainment produced for and aimed at the middle- and lower-class audiences was not altogether original and was often not accorded much scholarly or critical acclaim. Although it is not my intention to claim that these films are the same as nineteenth-century melodrama, they do share some contextual circumstances, and it is not surprising that producer/director George King brought adaptations of melodrama plays to the screen for a popular audience. Even these early "quota quickie" films contain messages and themes within the entertainment matrix.

For this study, I look at two stage melodramas that later became films. The story of the Murder of Maria Marten, also known as the Murder in the Red Barn, held audiences' attention for more than one hundred years. The events surrounding Maria Marten's murder in 1828 inspired multiple melodramas and eventually formed the basis for the 1935 film *The Murder in the Red Barn,* produced by George King and featuring Tod Slaughter in the villain's role. Better known today is the tale of Sweeney Todd, although it has changed in remarkable ways from its original stage appearance in George Dibdin-Pitt's 1847 drama. King and Slaughter continued their filmmaking partnership with a cinematic version of *Sweeney Todd* in 1936. While the films preserve some themes and characteristics from the original plays, there are significant changes as well. Where the Red Barn plays drew from life, the film versions drew from the theatre's representations of the story, further removing them from life. Although these movies are often categorized as early and original horror films, the filmmakers consciously reference the stories' histories, and significantly neutralize any real anxiety the audiences might feel, by employing theatrical framing techniques. Since the stories were repeated and altered over a century, I also address the problematic idea of "authenticity" by using terms "Red Barn–ness" and "Sweeney Todd–ness" to discuss what characteristics seem most essential and are most frequently preserved over time and through shifts in entertainment venue and format.

Maria Marten, or the Murder in the Red Barn

The Red Barn case provided raw material full of passion, seduction, sin, provincial life, family ties, and murder most foul. In the Suffolk countryside, in 1827, twenty-four-year-old William Corder murdered his lover, Maria Marten, and buried her body in a shallow grave in the floor of his family's red-roofed barn. In 1828, he was arrested in London and returned to Suffolk for trial. Before his trial commenced, the town of Polstead held its annual Cherry Fair, where the two most popular amusements were a camera obscura presentation of the murder and a booth theatre showing tableaux representations of the murder.[9]

This was an intensely popular case. As book author and London *Times* journalist James Curtis observed, the night before Corder's highly publicized trial was to begin, "such was the influx of visitors [to Bury] that many had to pay a guinea for a single bed, or to take no bed at all."[10] The fact that reporters could even get into the courtroom the following day was a small miracle. The pamphlet *Red Barn Tragedy!* informs its readers that "though every exertion was made . . . to facilitate the ingress of reporters, yet for a time they proved fruitless, and it was only by being actually hauled over the barriers that they reached the place allotted to them."[11] During the proceedings, court had to pause temporarily when one windowpane was shattered from the force of the crowds outside pressed against the glass.[12]

A unique convergence of the popular press and the moralizing sermon helped to keep the case in the public eye. The sermons used the case to exemplify the wages of sin, first in the case of Marten, who had sexual relationships outside of marriage, and finally in the case of Corder, who was executed for murder. The Rev. Charles Hyatt preached a sermon in the open air within view of the Red Barn itself, attracting tearful tourist crowds. When Corder was executed, the Rev. Meshach Seaman used the occasion to preach, and publish, a sermon on God's justice.[13]

Initial attempts by early audiences to consume the event resulted in a morbid tourist trade in and around the Suffolk town of Polstead, particularly at the site of the murder. Just over eighty miles from London, the provincial town was within a day's travel even for those on horseback. The victim's tombstone was chipped away to oblivion, boards from the Red Barn were ripped from the building and turned into snuff boxes, and the Staffordshire Pottery industry produced figurines of the murderer, victim, and the barn where the crime took place. Even the murderer's skin, skeleton, and hanging rope were all reconceived as souvenirs, items to be collected, to be held, and to be owned.[14]

In a matter of months, the story moved into the working-class London playhouses. It does us well to remember that a play performed for an audience, especially a paying audience in a commercial context, is also a commodity. The performance itself is a form of material culture, designed and presented to a consuming public. Further, as Tracy Davis has written, "The theatre organizes people and information. . . . It needs to be re-made for each performance, and fully exists only in the presence of consumers in the same space and time as the performers and operatives whose services are being expended."[15] By its very nature, theatre relies on the presence of the performers and the audience creating meaning together.

Shortly after Corder's execution in 1828, a version of the case was presented at the Royal Pavilion Theatre in the London suburb of Mile-End. One of the "illegitimate" London theatres, it offered melodramatic fare to working-class audiences. Surviving advertisements and journalist commentary indicate that other theatres across London were also presenting variations of the Red Barn case, but the only surviving script from the 1820s is *The Red Barn, or, the Mysterious Murder,* written for the Royal Pavilion by West Digges in 1828. When the script was published, it included a one-page author's preface reflecting on the success of the actors' performance in bringing these characters to life.[16]

The question of "authenticity" was important in the early crime-melodrama days, and the playwrights and theatres went to great lengths to proclaim their renderings "authentic." This was the logical extension of a trend perhaps epitomized by the 1824 efforts of Surrey Theatre manager Llewellyn "Boiled Beef" Williams, who staged the crime melodrama *The Gamblers* after purchasing the accused murderers' "identical horse and gig . . . together with the table at which the party supped, the sofa as described to having been slept on, with other household furniture."[17] To ensure authenticity for his Red Barn play, West Digges worked from a number of news reports, including the *London Times* articles by James Curtis. The playwright embedded references to actual people and details from the trial. As in life, Maria's family becomes concerned largely due to Mrs. Marten's disturbing dreams in which she envisions Maria's unholy burial. Mentions of William Corder's velveteen jacket are accurate. In one of the most infamous scenes from the life and the play, Maria dresses in men's clothing to sneak unrecognized across the fields, thinking she is meeting William so they could elope and marry far from his disapproving family. The playwright preserves "Red Barn–

ness" by setting the critical murder scene in the Red Barn, establishing the landlord/tenant relationship between the Marten and Corder families, and keeping the participants' names intact.

The play, however, also makes notable omissions and alterations. Maria's stepmother, who was only about two years older than Maria, is reconceived as "Dame Marten," her elderly natural mother. Maria's sister, Anne, is completely rewritten to be played by the theatre's leading comedienne, and Anne's entirely fictional fiancé, Tim Bobbin, is a stereotypical country bumpkin character. Despite the fact that all of the play's central characters are from a provincial setting, the comic characters exhibit rough language and bawdy humor that clearly sets them on a lower rung of the social ladder. David Grimsted, discussing character types across the genre of melodrama, observes that "all low-comedy stereotypes were presented on stage with some condescension as well as much affection."[18] This certainly seems to be the case with Digges's comic couple, who became entrenched in the Red Barn story. After this point, it was impossible to have a Red Barn story without the comic couple of Anne and Tim. All of these adjustments were made to bring the Marten/Corder story into alignment with the expectations of the audience and the conventions of melodrama. In life, Maria was not exactly a naïve victim seduced by a dastardly aristocrat. The fictional Maria was quietly rehabilitated to suit a black-and-white moral universe in which inherently good or inherently bad characters reign. The play includes a fleeting reference to one of Marten's lovers, his child, and his money, but the script does not provide context or explain that the reason Mr. Peter Mathews sent Maria an allowance of five pounds quarterly was because she had given birth to their illegitimate son three years earlier. Instead, the character of Maria is shown haunted by guilt for having a singular relationship with William. The play reinforces the ideal of the chaste young female by demonstrating through Maria's counterexample the pain and death that might be expected for a fallen woman who transgressed the gender-determined ideological paradigm.[19]

Elements of spectacle are also typical of melodramas. On stage, Maria's death by pistol shot is overshadowed by a haunting. Maria's spectacular ghost visits William in his prison cell before his execution, offering Christian forgiveness and urging him to repent and confess before his hanging. Although a haunting on stage can be presented in a fairly simple way, and is always shadowed by the audience's knowledge of the corporeal actor's real body, nineteenth-century theatres developed elaborate stage tricks for making ghosts appear and disappear, variously employing hidden ramps, trapdoors, harnesses for flying, bright lamps, and mirrors.

All of these alterations beg the question how a theatre could possibly have offered this as a true crime story, "authentic" in its details. The story had to be adjusted and molded, for time and dramatic effect, and to align with the audience's horizon of expectations. Surviving scripts from the 1850s and 1870s slowly but surely changed the Red Barn tale even more. There is an obvious and perhaps inevitable shift that occurs when material becomes divorced from its historical source, by time or distance, and is reinterpreted and adapted. Where other playwrights had quoted newspapers and sketched out situations, the later versions of the Red Barn story offered a more coherent and original plot at the expense of "authenticity."[20] These changes culminated in the kind of story eventually offered in film. Over time, the villain becomes an urbane landlord, while the victims and heroes are clearly the self-sufficient working farm folk who face disenfranchisement and hardship, and who must stand up to the corrupt member of the gentry to achieve justice. Although different in details, the later Red Barn dramas still share traits that preserve their Red Barn–ness: they still refer to the characters by name, include iconic events from the actual case such as the burial in the barn or Maria's appearance in breeches, focus on the actions of the villain, and center the action in the rural landscape.

Such Red Barn–ness is clearly present in the 1935 film *The Murder in the Red Barn,* even if the details differ considerably. Produced by George King, the movie features veteran stage actor Tod Slaughter as the murderous William and carries a byline for author Frederick Hayward. Although the script is heavily indebted to earlier dramatic versions, the plot and circumstances diverge in several significant ways. Gone is the famous breeches scene, gone are Maria's siblings, gone is Mrs. Marten's informative and graphic dream. The spectacle comes not from a haunting but in the form of elaborate and extended dance sequences. The film preserves the country-bumpkin couple of Anne and Tim, but here Anne is the Marten household servant. Mr. Marten is still a farmer, but he is now presented as a gentlemanly figure, rather than the struggling molecatcher he was in life, or the struggling tenant farmer created for earlier play scripts. William Corder is presented not as a bookish and impulsive twenty-four-year-old son of a squire, but as a mature and wealthy magistrate consumed by gambling and debts.[21] Another addition to the case is a band of gypsies—exotic and mysterious, misunderstood yet honorable, the gypsy Carlos is vainly in love with Maria and works tirelessly to uncover her murder. As Katie Trumpener explains, gypsy appearances in nineteenth-century fiction offered "fantasies in which individual or historical differences of experience within 'the Gypsy camp' are left deliberately undifferentiated and unexplored."[22] Gypsy characters might be, as Montagu Slater suggests, merely "a convention in Victorian melodramas. It was felt their presence brought a touch of poetry,"[23] and gypsies make an important appearance in a late-nineteenth-century version of the Red Barn story created by John Latimer for his touring company. The minor historical detail that gypsy people really did pass through Corder's Suffolk town is exploded into a central plot element for the film script. The gypsies do offer a kind of exotic touch, but as a noble yet disenfranchised member of a misunderstood people, Carlos is in an excellent position to capitalize on the audience's sympathies.

These radical departures from the original case make sense as steps in the evolution of the tale, but perhaps an even more interesting aspect of the film has to do with *how* the film presents the story. Immediately after the opening credits, the film shows not a serene countryside, but the inside of a theatre and the backs of the heads of people sitting, evidently, in the first or second row. A house manager steps onto the stage and, without ever looking into the camera, addresses the "audience" present within view. Against a painted backdrop, the manager introduces each of the major characters, who cross the stage and bow or curtsy in turn. The parade includes the age-worn and proud father, the mother with her noble gray hairs, the lovely Maria, and the mystery hangman, cloaked and hidden from view. Despite the film audience's physical presence in front of a film screen, the filmmakers position the story as a dramatic fiction, and distance the audience from the events by establishing a theatrical framework.

The film plays up the sexual relationship between Maria and William, and divorced from the need to maintain a sense of authenticity, it capitalizes on the late melodramatic tension between corrupt wealth and honest poverty. Lured by the prospect of marriage, provincial Maria has a sexual relationship with William and clearly becomes pregnant, despite the fact that the word is never explicitly stated in the film. The lurking gypsies, outsiders motivated by a need for revenge in Latimer's script, become agents of justice in the film. Carlos the gypsy works alongside the police, another nod to the mid-nineteenth-century melodramas that glorified the newly formalized police force and the professional officer of the law.

Even early films enjoy some technological advantages over theatrical production: where the play script calls for short scenes, or scenes occurring one after another, the film is able to cut back and forth, as in the simultaneous action of Dame Marten saying her prayers while William shoots Maria and buries her body. The camera's point of view enables the spectator to sit high above the dance floor, marveling at the patterns of the country dances, or to move effortlessly from exterior to interior. The camera allows close-up shots of faces and shifting expressions that might be lost to audiences in a large playhouse. The film, however, demonstrates a fascinating debt to stage acting in the gestures employed by almost every actor. Presumably more subtle than the declamatory stage conventions of a century earlier, they nevertheless recall physical performance training; actors strike poses that include a hand over the heart, a comic waddling walk, clasped pleading hands, or a hand to the forehead. The movements seem appropriate, because they so well suit the characters, and artificial, in that they are obviously choreographed and not natural postures.

The film is, in detail, a far cry from the original case. But the Red Barn–ness is preserved. Maria's death is framed as tragic punishment for her moral lapse and is shattering to the wholesome provincial community. The murder is executed in a perfectly rendered barn. And, ultimately, justice prevails. Carlos the gypsy steps in as the substitute executioner, and the camera dwells on William's feet standing on the gallows trapdoor. A drumroll begins, and then the closing credit appears on screen. In the final moments, the audience is, somewhat unsatisfactorily, denied a return to the theatrical motif that might be expected given the film's opening sequence "inside" a playhouse. It is as if the movie had started with a theatre script but taken a journey to create a consciously filmic product.

Sweeney Todd

The Red Barn stories, although popular with working-class theatre audiences and early filmmakers, are not well known to most people today. Far more recognizable is the tale of Sweeney Todd. Perhaps the most enduring murder melodrama, the legend of Sweeney Todd was dramatized by George Dibdin-Pitt in 1847 as *The String of Pearls: The Fiend of Fleet Street.* When it opened at the Britannia Theatre on February 22, 1847, it, too, was advertised as being "Founded on Fact," despite the fact that official records do not show any barber named Todd or any barbershop in Fleet Street or even any barbershop-over-a-pie-shop in any street at all.[24] Generations of armchair historians have attempted to track down the "real" Sweeney Todd, but he is a mythical figure. In fact, the story seems to have originated from an 1825 French short story titled "A Terrible Story of the Rue de la Harpe," popularized by Thomas Peckett Prest through penny dreadful installments in 1847.[25] In 1936, George King and Tod Slaughter again teamed up to film a cinema version of *Sweeney Todd.*

The basic tenets of Dibdin-Pitt's play and the King/Slaughter film are the same. A murderous, avaricious barber named Sweeney Todd kills men and takes their money or jewels to line his own pockets. The victims are then turned into meat pies by the barber's neighbor, Mrs. Lovett. The two are discovered when Sweeney Todd unwisely targets a resourceful sea captain. In both cases, Sweeney Todd meets his end when the sailor forces him into his own murderous barber's chair.

In the play, the multiple subplots are relatively complex, including a suitor for Mrs. Lovett, several unique murders, the rescue of an apprentice unjustly committed to an insane asylum, and the misfortunes of an eyeglasses maker and his daughter. The potential perils faced by lovers are less important than the treatment of apprentices and the struggles of working men. In the play, Sweeney Todd thinks he has killed sailor Mark Ingestrie, but Mark survives his fall from the booby-trapped barber's chair and escapes. Sweeney Todd is brought before the court at the end of act 3, but he mistakes the not-actually-dead Mark Ingestrie for a ghost, loses his wits, and breaks out of jail. In an elaborate showdown at the end of the play, Mark reunites with his sweetheart Johanna, tracks Sweeney to his barbershop, and engages in a fistfight. Mark's male friends arrive, the men force Sweeney into his own barber chair, and he "falls to the depths below."[26]

The film begins with an introductory frame, but of a more cinematic nature than found in the Red Barn film. In the early 1930s, a customer walks into a barbershop, casually inquiring about a plaque on the wall. The barber then begins to tell him the story of Sweeney Todd, which he claims occurred one hundred years earlier on that same spot, and the film proper begins. This deliberate shift to an earlier period puts the film in the same spirit as the original play. Although written in the 1840s, the play script is specifically set in the reign of King George II. It seems that whenever this script is written, its central events are deliberately set roughly a century earlier.

The time shift gimmick has several effects, one of which was to assure the mid-nineteenth-century audience that such terrible events were things of the past and would not happen in the newly civilized and organized London. Another was to excuse the lack of police or detective work in the play. The police, in most murder melodramas, serve as a sort of deus ex machina, where the human figure of the officer of the law replaces the god from the machine. If it is the king in *Tartuffe* who served as the all-seeing, all-knowing agent of justice, it is the working officer of the law who eventually became the nineteenth-century agent actively tasked with assuring that justice is done. While there is a marked lack of interest in the sleuthing process, the villain's guilt is a foregone conclusion since the audience witnesses the crime, so no other suspects need to be considered. When the figure of the lawman is absent, as in the case of *Sweeney Todd*, it is by design. By demonstrating the failings of the previous century's incomprehensible justice system and incompetent or absent police force, nineteenth-century melodrama reinforced the need for, and appreciation of, the modern law-enforcement system. Nineteenth-century Londoners were eager to dismiss the previous century as a more barbaric time. "The law of England was not deliberately formulated with conscious social purpose. It accumulated capriciously," writes Sandra Lee Kerman in her introduction to selections from *The Newgate Calendar*. Before 1688, there were about fifty classes of felonies. By the start of the nineteenth century, there were over two hundred. Laws were frequently passed in response to a particular incident, and the result was that "trivial and major crimes alike were often capital offenses." For instance, in the 1700s, it was a felony, punishable by death, to steal fruit that had been harvested, but it was only a misdemeanor to pick fruit oneself and steal it.[27]

The system was badly in need of both reform and regulation, which slowly began to take shape throughout the nineteenth century. A new police force was initially introduced in London in 1828. In 1829, just a year after the Red Barn case, the Metropolitan Police Act was passed, conferring authority on a centralized, uniformed police force. The new "unified force, replacing the hodgepodge system of parish watchmen," consisted of five divisions, each with inspectors, sergeants, and 144 constables all tasked with learning his own "beat"; all were ultimately answerable to the British Home Secretary, Robert Peele.[28] Parliament passed other legal acts, as well, designed to clarify the criminal code and provide the law-enforcement agents nationwide with the tools needed to establish order. The new police force also needed a new literature, such as *Instructions to the New Police* and the *Constable's Pocket Companion and Guide,* published in 1829 and 1830 respectively.[29] The contrast between the civilizing forces of the newly accepted policeman and the chaotic past also positions the common working-class sailor as an acceptable hero in lawless places, administering justice as he saw fit. A similar shift presumably works with the film, since the undifferentiated pseudo-Victorian period it presents is noticeably devoid of police or authority figures.

The central portion of the film, however, follows much the same story as the play, while eliminating most of the subplots. Johanna's father, originally a spectacle maker, is reconceived as a wealthy shipping tycoon, and the sailor Mark, Johanna's true love, is too poor to be considered a worthy suitor and therefore sets to sea. While Mark is away at sea, Johanna spends most of the film fending off Sweeney's lecherous advances. The film cuts fluidly between London and events on Mark's ship, the *Golden Hope*. The first truly spectacular moment shows the African outpost where Trader Patterson, awaiting the arrival of the *Golden Hope,* is beset by native Africans. Trader Patterson's loyal African servant (a very attractive actor apparently of African descent, and the only character to show a well-muscled chest through a torn shirt) runs to the shore and, almost drowning in the process, alerts the men aboard the ship who rush to the trader's rescue. When the ship's captain is killed in the skirmish, Mark is promoted to captain and a fortune in pearls passes into his hands. Mark returns to London as a wealthy man and makes the mistake of allowing Sweeney Todd, who meets him at the dock, to talk him into a shave. Mrs. Lovett rightly suspects that Sweeney is going to swindle her out of her half of the earnings, so when Mark Ingestrie drops through the barber's trapdoor, Mrs. Lovett acts out of spite by hiding Mark and helping him escape through underground passageways.

In the final showdown, Johanna, trying to get a full sense of the situation, dresses as a boy and asks for apprentice work at Sweeney's shop, but he clocks her over the head and stuffs her in a cabinet, with plans to "polish her off" later. Sweeney meets Mrs. Lovett in their shared cellar, kills her, and sets fire to both their shops, but Mark and a cadre of intrepid sailors arrive in time for Mark to rescue Johanna, have a wrestling match with the razor-wielding Sweeney, and eventually throw Sweeney into his own evil barber's chair. The raging smoke and fire are another truly spectacular element. No matter how much a theatre audience might accept the scenic special effects of a fire, the camera's ability to capture the real thing on film imparts a realistic element the stage perhaps cannot match. Perhaps one reason why the censor's office allowed the release of the sensational King/Slaughter films was that the most hideous crimes occur just outside of the camera's frame. When Sweeney attacks victims, his main modus operandi is cracking them over the head with chairs. The demon barber's chair, activated by a lever, turns over the whole section of the floor, dumping the bodies of Sweeney Todd's victims into the basement, alive but unconscious, to be polished off later and out of view.

Sweeney Todd–ness is well preserved between the stage and the film. The basics of the story are quite striking on their own, and surely the barbaric and shocking idea of a murderer baking victims into pies, thereby committing the unsuspecting public to acts of cannibalism, helped make the story particularly memorable. A film scene in which a clueless sailor munches on one of Mrs. Lovett's pies while wondering where the bodies are hidden echoes a play script scene in which a clueless would-be shop assistant munches a pie. The Sweeney Todd film also preserves some of the same kinds of melodramatic acting conventions that the Red Barn film presented. A young apprentice pleads with Sweeney by grasping

Sweeney Todd's arm and swooning, Johanna's distressed father pauses to drop his head and pinch the bridge of his nose, while Johanna's maid moves with a comic awkwardness that requires her to hike up her skirts and bounce her shoulders in a caricaturish way.

In both play and film, the villain's actions drive the play forward, but the hero sailor blessed with bravery, good luck, and ingenuity is a true staple of British stage melodrama. The Adelphi Theatre, in fact, made its reputation on producing nautical melodramas celebrating the patriotic British seaman.[30] Versions of the Sweeney Todd play were presented throughout nineteenth-century London, usually in working-class minor theatres or puppet theatres, but it seems that the story never claimed to be an account of contemporary events.[31] Slaughter's film, which opened with the story-telling twentieth-century barber, closes with a return to the same frame story that subverts the film's horror with a comic moment in which the modern customer, frightened by the story, slips from the barber's chair and runs out into the street with lather still on his face.

Sweeney Todd's tale continues to change. Most present-day audiences are familiar with Sweeney Todd because he is the subject of a famous and critically acclaimed, Tony Award–winning musical by Stephen Sondheim, *Sweeney Todd: The Demon Barber of Fleet Street.* However, Sondheim's source is not a nineteenth-century script, but rather a free adaptation written in the 1970s by Christopher Bond in an attempt to update and flesh out the classic British murder tale. A major Hollywood film version of the musical, released on December 21, 2007, by Dreamworks and Warner Brothers Pictures, with director Tim Burton and A-list leading man Johnny Depp, furthered the reach of the Sondheim/Bond version. The recent movie's Sweeney Todd–ness echoes back to the original stage play, with Sweeney's strange makeup, his habit of murdering victims in his barber's chair, an ill-treated apprentice, and Mrs. Lovett's conveniently located meat pie shop. But Bond provided his characters with significant new back stories, relationships, psychologies, and motivations completely absent from the previous century's play script. Each time a new generation retells an old story, the storyteller owes a debt to the storytellers of the past, but the story must also shift to meet the desires of the new era.

Conclusion

The hour-long feature films starring Tod Slaughter as a melodramatic villain and produced by George King, recorded on Vistatone under license from Marconi's Wireless Telegraph Company, Ltd., are probably not "great works of art." But, then, neither were their source materials.

What we do know is that crime melodramas, like melodramas in general, played to great numbers of people over the course of the nineteenth century. The number of British murder dramas, whether true-crime or fiction, exploded in the first half of the nineteenth century; there are at least seventy nineteenth-century plays with the word "murder" in the title, and twenty-five of these were produced between 1821 and 1840.[32] A popular, commercial theatrical production was a commodity, and the attending play scripts, printed and sold, were also commodities, although of a slightly different nature. To rapidly produce audience-pleasing plays, melodrama playwrights worked from a variety of sources, including literature, folk tales, adventure epics, established scenarios, and real-life events. The presence of the catchphrase "Founded on Fact" for even such a fictional figure as Sweeney Todd is one indicator of the power this advertising construction could command. The nineteenth-century melodrama theatre was not at all shy about borrowing from other sources. In the 1930s in England, the early commercial film industry also searched for adaptable material, and it is probably inevitable that some producers would turn to little-known but once popular plays for their sources. The British "quota quickie" films recycled existing plots in a way that was not so different from the reworking of stories for the theatre's melodrama audiences about a century earlier.

Besides preserving some essential Red Barn–ness or Sweeney Todd–ness, these representations are geared to work on the sympathies of a popular audience. In the nineteenth century, at a time when public executions were still great tourist attractions, the representation and dramatic repetition of horrible acts were not generally considered offensive, especially when the tale concluded with a clear moral lesson and the glorification of solid principles of the rising English middle class: family devotion, hard work, sobriety, justice, and religious piety. In melodramas, the virtuous receive their reward whether in this world or the next, and evildoers are punished by law, by their own guilty consciences, or by an act of God. In the 1930s, the censor's office seemed inclined to pass early horror films like the King/Slaughter movies when the films showed consequences for immoral acts. The Red Barn story, on stage and in film, capitalizes on perceived tensions between male and female, innocence and debauchery, rogue actions and the professionalized police, and significantly between the ignoble rich and the disenfranchised poor, even if the identity and social background of the specific sympathetic hero shifted over time. Sweeney Todd tales from the nineteenth and early twentieth centuries also offer a working-class hero in the adventurous British sailor. Additionally, Dibdin-Pitt's early Sweeney Todd melodrama establishes a pseudo-historical period for the play's events, and the King/Slaughter film gives the audience an almost voyeuristic thrill by looking into a barbaric past, efforts that consequently neutralize Sweeney Todd's threat and highlight the civilized nature of the current age, whatever that current age happened to be.

It is interesting to assess the similarities and differences between melodrama play scripts and later related film artifacts. It is just as useful to tease out how they present their entertainments as it is to chart the twists and turns each story has taken. Theatre- and filmmakers have engaged in processes of borrowing and adapting since the drama began, and the process of telling and retelling crime stories, old and new, continues today.

Notes

1. For more on this, see Pierre Bourdieu, *The Field of Cultural Production: Essays on Art and Literature* (New York: Columbia University Press, 1993), 217–19. Bourdieu observed that it is only because of our accumulated education and ability to interpret multiple levels of signification that we might stumble across Da Vinci's *The Last Supper* and recognize it as anything more than a rendering of twelve men at a dinner table.

2. Richard Leacroft, *The Development of the English Playhouse* (London: Methuen, 1988), 166. See also Rand Carter, "The Drury Lane Theatres of Henry Holland and Benjamin Dean Wyatt," *Journal of the Society of Architectural Historians* 26, no. 3 (October 1967): 209–14.

3. Michael Hays and Anastasia Nikolopoulou, introduction to *Melodrama: The Cultural Emergence of a Genre* (New York: St Martin's Press, 1996), viii.

4. Michael Booth, "The Social and Literary Context," in *The Revels History of Drama in English, 1750–1880* (London: Methuen, 1975), 48–49. Booth writes that even the venerable Drury Lane was unwilling or unable to pay its best writers what their contracts demanded. Drury Lane initially offered four hundred pounds to playwright James Kenney for a play called *Masaniello,* but in 1832 the theatre was bankrupt and Kenney received no money at all, despite the fact that *Masaniello* played for over 150 nights.

5. Booth, "Social and Literary Context," 50.

6. Thomas J. Taylor, "Cumberland, Kotzebue, Scribe, Simon: Are We Teaching the Wrong Playwrights?" *College English* 43, no. 1 (January 1981): 46. Taylor observes that academic authors treat plays with more respect when they read them as literary works, regardless of their popularity on stage.

7. Thomas Postlewait, "From Melodrama to Realism: The Suspect History of American Drama," in *Melodrama: The Cultural Emergence of a Genre,* ed. Hays and Nikolopoulou, 54–55.

8. Lawrence Napper, "Review: Steve Chibnall, '*Quota Quickies*': *The Birth of the British 'B' Film,*" *Screen* 48, no. 4 (Winter 2007): 551. A "quota quickie"

was usually a short British feature film, produced on a limited budget and in a very short time frame, in order to satisfy government regulations that British film studios release a minimum number of films per year to combat the influx of movies from the United States. Between 1930 and 1940, commercial filmmaker George King directed or produced sixty-nine films.

9. J. (James) Curtis, *An Authentic and Faithful History of the Mysterious Murder of Maria Marten with a Full Development of all the Extraordinary Circumstances Which Led to the Discovery of Her Body in The Red Barn; to Which Is Added, the Trial of William Corder, Taken at Large in Short Hand Specially for This Work, with an Account of His Execution, Dissection, &c., and Many Interesting Particulars Relative to the Village of Polstead and Its Vicinity; The Prison Correspondence of Corder, and Fifty-Three Letters, in Answer to His Advertisement for a Wife* (London: Thomas Kelly, 1828), 55–56.

10. Curtis, *Mysterious Murder,* 83.

11. Anonymous, *The Red Barn Tragedy! An Authentic Narrative of the Atrocious Murder of Maria Marten: Giving Full Particulars of the Miraculous Discovery of the Body in the Red Barn, Polstead: And Also the Trial of William Corder, for the Said Murder, at Bury on Thursday and Friday, August 7 & 8, 1828, before Mr. Baron Alexander, with an Account of his Execution,* 3rd ed. (Southwark: G. Smeeton and G. H. Davidson, 1828), 3.

12. Curtis, *Mysterious Murder,* 142–43.

13. Charles Hyatt, *The Sinner Detected: A Sermon Preached in the Open Air, near the Red Barn at Polstead, and the Meeting-House, Boxford, Suffolk, and in the Afternoon and Evening of Sunday, the 17th of August, 1828, on Occasion of the Execution of William Corder for the Murder of Maria Marten, Including Particulars of His Life Never before Published* (London: Westley and Davis, 1828); Rev. M. (Meshach) Seaman, *The Privileges of the Righteous and the Woes of the Wicked, A Sermon Delivered in the Parish Church of East Donyland, Sunday Morning, August 17, 1828, and Repeated, by Desire, in the Afternoon of the Same Day at St. Peter's Church, Colchester, on the Occasion of the Execution of William Corder, for Murder* (Ipswich: S. Piper, 1828). Hyatt's sermon is held at the British Library in London. Seaman's sermon is in the Rare Books collection at the Library of Congress Law Library in Washington, DC.

14. Curtis, *Mysterious Murder,* 55–56; "The Red Barn at Polstead," *London Times,* July 31, 1828. Examples of some of the souvenirs, including the Red Barn pottery figures, are held at the Moyses Hall Museum in St. Edmundsbury, England http://www.stedmundsbury.gov.uk/sebc/visit/exhibits.cfm.

15. Tracy Davis, *The Economics of the British Stage, 1800–1914* (Cambridge: Cambridge University Press, 2000), 334.

16. West Digges, *The Red Barn, or, the Mysterious Murder: A Melo-Drama in Two Acts: Founded on the Late Melancholy Transaction Which Took Place at the Village of Polstead, 18th May 1827* (London: Teulon and Fox, 1828). Those seeking the script may use call number KD372.C665 C665 1828 LL TRIALS, and will need to make a special appointment with the Rare Books curator at the Law Library reading room of the Library of Congress. The West Digges script is bound

along with newspaper clippings and an 1828 first edition of J. (James) Curtis's seminal book on the case, published by Thomas Kelly of London.

17. Advertisement, "New Surrey Theatre Re-Production of The Gamblers," January 15, 1824. Original image reproduced in Albert Borowitz, *The Thurtell-Hunt Murder Case: Dark Mirror to Regency England* (Baton Rouge: Louisiana State University Press, 1987), 129.

18. David Grimsted, *Melodrama Unveiled: American Theater and Culture, 1800–1850* (Chicago: University of Chicago Press, 1968), 194.

19. For more on the lessons of propriety and gender, particularly with regards to French melodramas, see Léon Metayer, "What the Heroine Taught, 1830–1870," in *Melodrama: The Cultural Emergence of a Genre,* ed. Hays and Nikolopoulou, 235–44.

20. Examples of such extant scripts: Anonymous, "Maria Martin [*sic*], or the Murder in the Red Barn," *The Golden Age of Melodrama,* ed. Michael Kilgarriff (London: Wolfe Publishing, 1974), and John Latimer, *Maria Marten, or Murder in the Red Barn,* ed. Montagu Slater, 2nd ed. (London: Heinemann Education Books, 1971).

21. The increased age of the villain may also be related to the actor's situation. Slaughter was about age fifty at the time of the filming.

22. Katie Trumpener, "The Time of the Gypsies: A 'People without History' in the Narratives of the West," *Critical Inquiry* 18, no. 4, Identities (Summer 1992): 847.

23. Slater, introduction to *Maria Marten, or Murder in the Red Barn,* viii.

24. See Robert L. Mack, *The Wonderful and Surprising History of Sweeney Todd: The Life and Times of an Urban Legend* (London: Continuum, 2007); Albert Borowitz, *Blood and Ink: An International Guide to Fact-Based Crime Literature* (Kent, OH: Kent State University Press, 2002); and Richard D. Altick, *Victorian Studies in Scarlet* (New York: W. W. Norton, 1970).

25. Mack, *Wonderful and Surprising History of Sweeney Todd.* See also "PBS Presents Sweeney Todd, the Demon Barber of Fleet Street in Concert: A String of Pearls," http://www.pbs.org/kqed/demonbarber/play/index.html.

26. George Dibdin-Pitt, *Sweeney Todd: The Demon Barber of Fleet Street,* ed. Montagu Slater (London: Percy Lund Humphreys and Co. for John Lane the Bodley Head, 1951), 79.

27. Sandra Lee Kerman, introduction to *The Newgate Calendar, or Malefactor's Bloody Register* (New York: Capricorn Books, 1962), viii–xi.

28. From *Bell's Weekly Messenger,* October 4, 1829, quoted in Ginny Crosthwait, "*They Belong to Ourselves!*": *Criminal Proximity in Nineteenth Century British Narrative and Culture* (PhD diss., Rice University, 2004), 26.

29. James Shaw, *Constable's Pocket Companion and Guide, Containing the Duties, Powers, Responsibilities, Indemnity, Remuneration, and Expenses of Those Officers* (London: Sherwood, Gilbert, and Piper, 1830); Anonymous, *Instructions to the New Police* (London: Marsh and Miller, 1829).

30. Michael Booth, "Soldiers of the Queen: Drury Lane Imperialism," in *Melodrama: The Cultural Emergence of a Genre,* ed. Hays and Nikolopoulou, 3–4.

31. An American stage version of *Sweeney Todd* was published around 1852. In 1860, London's Pavilion Theatre submitted an anonymous adaptation seeking the approval of the Lord Chamberlain as official censor. Three new versions of the Sweeney Todd story were performed at various theatres around London in 1861, with two more the following year. Authorial attributions, if not extant scripts, survive today for eight separate versions dramatized in 1865, mostly for provincial English theatres. The Royal Victoria Theatre became known as "the bleedin' Vic" because of the number of murder plays produced there, particularly *Sweeney Todd.* See Mack, *Wonderful and Surprising History of Sweeney Todd,* 246–354, and James L. Smith, *Melodrama* (London: Methuen, 1973), 42.

32. Altick, *Victorian Studies in Scarlet,* 88.

Robert Edmond Jones

Theatre and Motion Pictures, Bridging Reality and Dreams

Anthony Hostetter and Elisabeth Hostetter

SCHOLARS CREDIT Robert Edmond Jones with starting a revolution in American theatre on January 27, 1915, with his integrated design work on *The Man Who Married a Dumb Wife*. Jones defined the "New Stagecraft" of the United States by seamlessly uniting the visual components of set, light, and costume design to underscore the director's concept and highlight the actor on stage. He later articulated his motivations, creative process, and visions for theatre in public lectures and published articles. In 1941, he published the collected essays in *The Dramatic Imagination,* a book often considered required reading for students of the theatre.

The Dramatic Imagination advocates a unified style that Brooks Atkinson refers to as "poetic idealism." In an article commemorating the release of Jones's book, subtitled "Notes on the Case of Robert Edmond Jones, the Scene Designer Who Keeps His Own Faith through the Years," Atkinson wrote of Jones: "Like a true New Englander, his is of the Emersonian faith and believes in the over-soul. Beyond the literal detail that the eye sees he believes in vast resources of beauty that we can absorb through our senses, and he has always striven to catch fragments of it in his many works for the stage."[1] Jones's essays and lectures speak of the value of poetic idealism, but he also articulates goals and the potential that he sees for the future of American theatre. He started to philosophically contemplate the ideal and potential of dramatic presentation early in his career and attempted to practically stage his vision for the theatre of the future in his 1921 production of *Macbeth.* Ultimately, after going into psychotherapy with Carl Jung, Jones came to more fully understand the practical mechanics of how to stage poetic idealism, and he published those theoretical findings in *The Dramatic Imagination*. In order to decode and understand his vision as accurately as possible, it is important to read this seminal work within the context of Jones's practical stage work, his other writing, and his significant outside influences.

A 1952 audio recording of Jones transcribed and published by Delbert Unruh in 1992 called "The Theatre of the Future" is of primary interest in this paper. In his lecture circuit, Jones elaborated on a comment printed in *The Dramatic Imagination* in which he blamed blandly realistic design on society's fascination with photography. He claimed that fixation on naturalism would ultimately cause audiences to abandon theatre for motion pictures. Nevertheless, he firmly believed theatre would reawaken when it eventually integrated some of the advantages of motion pictures: "The new drama will display not only action but the thoughts which prompts the action—not only the deed but the emotion behind the deed. . . . Objective experience will be interpreted by flesh-and-blood actors appearing on a stage which will resemble, more or less closely, the realistic stage we are familiar with today. But above and behind, and around this stage a motion picture screen will be erected. And on it are thrown the shadow selves of the characters of the drama—living and moving as our thoughts and emotion live and move."[2]

This study explores Jones's frustration with realism and his efforts to more clearly realize, articulate, and actualize his vision of the theatre of the future. While Jones spoke and wrote about the practical application of poetic idealism, he ultimately came to view it as a therapeutic way to dramatize a psychological concept that he felt drove and united all of humanity. Psychologist Carl Jung's notion of the power of the collective unconscious and his belief in the potential of art to present and decode symbols as a means to unite our conscious and subconscious minds strongly informed Jones's vision for the arts. After intensive, prolonged psychotherapy, Jones eventually came to believe that theatre's larger purpose was to help humanity come to terms with the power of the collective unconscious. We argue that Jones viewed the materiality of the human body on stage as a metaphor for the conscious mind and the fluid potential of film as the subtle background of the unconscious. We trace the development of Jones's work as a practical designer and theoretician that lead to his vision for the theatre of the future that he articulated toward the end of his career.

The "New Stagecraft" refers to production practices started in Europe and inspired by Adolph Appia and Edward Gordon Craig. Jones was certainly aware of Craig's work. Craig's periodical *The Mask* appeared in 1908, and his book, *The Art of the Theatre,* was available in 1911. In 1912, Max Reinhardt presented his production of *Sumurûn* on

Broadway, providing American audiences and Jones with their first glimpse of European-style stagecraft.[3] Jones put New Stagecraft theories into practice when he designed John Reed's 1913 *Paterson Strike Pageant* at Madison Square Garden and, according to one source, he "insisted on making it a Gordon Craig affair."[4] Immediately after the pageant, Jones sailed to Florence with the financial assistance of the "Robert Edmond Jones Transportation and Development Corporation" financed by Mabel Dodge and her salon of many artists and literary figures of the beginning of the twentieth century and many of Jones's classmates from Harvard. His ultimate goal was to secure an apprenticeship with Edward Gordon Craig.

Jones arrived at Craig's doorstep in the summer of 1913 but reported that the senior artist "refused to take me into his school because he had a quarrel with [Mabel Dodge]—I think he's doing wonderful stuff here—but personally he's a tiny man."[5] However, with a letter of support from a colleague of Max Reinhardt, Jones went to the Deutsches Theater Berlin to observe the work of other European designers.[6] Jones held no official position in Reinhardt's theatre; he was neither a student nor an assistant. He did, however, learn about the workings of a busy repertory company and he witnessed the practical application of Craig's and Appia's ideas on stage. Jones had the opportunity to see numerous productions during his tenure in Berlin, including a dozen newly staged works by Shakespeare.[7] Reinhardt had earned international fame with his vision for staging classical work because, as J. L. Styan has put it, "[Reinhardt] established what many thought to be the characteristic style of Shakespearian performance for the twentieth century—free flowing, highly rhythmic, leaning towards a symbolist use of color and design, seeking the right visual images for each play's mood and atmosphere, and catching the most telling emphasis in action and characterization."[8] Jones observed how Reinhardt's productions fused the artistic use of scenery, lighting, and costumes to create and enhance the mood and rhythm of the spoken drama. Although he admired the symbolic use of color and design, Jones ultimately believed that a simpler, less spectacular approach could likewise create the appropriate atmosphere for Shakespeare and allow for a more fluid and focused sense of drama.

Jones described how Max Reinhardt collaboratively worked with the actors, designers, and composer throughout the rehearsal process for the production of *Sumurûn* in a 1917 article titled "The Future Decorative Art of the Theatre." The result, according to Jones, was an integrated performance in which all the elements of the production supported the work of the actors on stage. Jones wished to see that process instituted in the Broadway theatre. He wanted actors, directors, designers, and playwrights to work together from initial idea through completion of a new production so that every element would combine to create a unified whole. The scenery developed in this process, as Jones put it, "should be so important that the audience should forget that it is painted. There should be a fusion between the play and its scenery. Scenery isn't there to be looked at, it's really there to be forgotten."[9] Even in his earliest articulation of a new design process, Jones defined scenery of his modified version of the New Stagecraft as part of the subconscious experience of theatre.

Kenneth Macgowan echoed this desire for unified theatre production in his 1919 article, "The New Path of the Theatre," but also sought to refine the ideas behind the New Stagecraft. Macgowan believed that the New Stagecraft fights against realism to produce stage design that has meaning and fits into the fabric of the drama. The New Stagecraft highlighted visual elements and promoted three essential concepts necessary to visually reveal the expressiveness of the play: simplification, suggestion, and synthesis. "Simplifying" the effects requires designers to clearly identify and delineate only the essential elements capable of expressing the intent of the drama. In addition, the designer must use limited elements on stage so that the actor takes precedence in the stage picture and is properly seen. "Suggestion" is the best way to amplify simplification because it points to a symbolic, yet universally understood, stage picture. For instance, the designer can use shadows of branches to represent a forest rather than reproducing every tree. Integrated design should suggest a forest and also evoke the mood expressed in the spoken drama. The third element, "synthesis," requires designers to ensure that all visual elements carefully coordinate, fit the intention of the play, and support the actors. All elements should blend to depict a cohesive, emotional, theatrical world instead of simply mimicking the mundane world.[10]

While Jones's commercial design practices generally remained grounded in key, recognizable elements that directly corresponded to the conscious, "real" world, his 1915 Broadway debut stressed the importance he placed on simplification, suggestion, and synthesis. Because New Stagecraft focuses on carefully considered, sparsely presented, essential, universal elements, it naturally emphasizes the importance of the symbolic use of scenery in the theatre. Jones's understanding of symbolism and the role the unconscious played in the theatre and art exponentially grew after he started psychotherapy with Dr. Smith-Ely Jelliffe around 1920.[11] Dr. Jelliffe, who collected a massive library on psychoanalysis, contributed greatly to America's understanding of Freud, Adler, and Jung through his publication of translated articles in a journal he cofounded called the *Psy-*

choanalytic Review. Jelliffe also authored over four hundred publications during his lifetime.[12] Jones's experience in therapy seriously impacted his views and practice of theatre and led to a greater emphasis on his evolution of symbolic design practices. This influence is especially evident in his design work for a 1921 production of *Macbeth.* Donald Oenslager, who apprenticed with Jones and became a lifelong friend, noted this about Jones's design for *Macbeth:* "Jones was deeply concerned with psychoanalysis and his brief suggestions of these scenes for *Macbeth* resembled personified abstractions, indications of place seen through the mind's eye of the characters of the play. In the letter scene . . . Lady Macbeth found her way, as in her own dream world."[13]

Arthur Hopkins, who directed the show and was likewise seeking psychotherapy, worked collaboratively with Jones to stage a radical version of *Macbeth* in which the conscious world was in a visual and visceral battle with the unconscious world on the stage. Hopkins must have anticipated the controversy and confusion this production would cause, because he published a dramaturgical essay in the *New York Times* two weeks before the February 17, 1921, opening of the Broadway production. He explained his view that Macbeth was "possessed" and "becomes as one in a dream." He likewise felt that Lady Macbeth was possessed and ultimately not rationally responsible for her actions. Hopkins explained, "we all have our unconscious devils," and he claimed that the tragedy of *Macbeth* is that strong people can be overtaken by forces they do not understand, which leads to their ultimate destruction. He explained: "We care nothing about how Inverness may have looked, neither do we care about all the conscious motives that have been ascribed to Macbeth and Lady Macbeth. We believe them all to be of no importance, because we believe the real causes were deeper seated than conscious motive, and, furthermore, that the same causes exist today in all people." Hopkins concludes the article by stating, "as to the settings, we have left behind all compromise with realism. There are just the barest beginnings of things. We believe there will be great beauty."[14] In a separate publication, Hopkins remarked on the dreamlike quality of Jones's design sketches by explaining: "They permitted an expanse of ominous witch-infested space. Figures came out of the dark into the light and were enveloped by the dark again. There was the quality of an evil dream in which visible objects had a nightmarish distortion. There was no sense of reality. The whole was pervaded by the poisonous brew of the witches' cauldron."[15]

Jones started with a vast, void, open, black platform on the proscenium stage of the Apollo Theatre on 42nd Street. He then added a gray fragment suggesting gothic arches that Alexander Woollcott later dispar-

Robert Edmond Jones's scene design for the banquet scene from *Macbeth*. Special Collections and Archive, Wesleyan University Library.

agingly described as reminiscent of a "giant molar tooth."[16] This "tooth" was replaced by other scenic elements during the play but, according to Woollcott, one symbol dominated the design: "The curtain rises on a black curtained stage of infinite depth and height. Glaring down on the center are three five-foot masks of dull silver. The eyes of these masks focus on a ring around which stand three indeterminate figures in crimson crepe. These red and midnight hags wear masks of bronze."[17] The bronze masks worn by the three witches were identical to the masks hung over the stage. Hopkins described the masks as a symbol intended to express the "unconscious devils." This idea stems directly from psychoanalyst Carl Jung's belief that symbols are the primary way for humans to express and acknowledge the contents of the unconscious: "What we call a symbol is a term, a name, or even a picture that may be familiar in daily life, yet that possesses specific connotations in addition to its conventional and obvious meaning. It implies something vague, unknown, or hidden from us."[18] The witches were intended to be a conscious, embodied connection to the suspended, enlarged, overhead masks that correspondingly represented the unconscious, internal forces that control the destiny of Macbeth.

Despite Jones's and Hopkins's best intentions, critics uniformly panned the production. Woollcott wrote no less than three reviews condemning the design of *Macbeth.* After the opening, he wrote, "[Jones's] blasted heath . . . suggests nothing so much as the lodge room of the Ku Klux Klan, Poughkeepsie Chapter."[19] Two days later, he wrote, "the attention was distracted by Mr. Jones, who in an effort to clear all of the old rubbishy 'scenic effects' out of the great play's way, was himself forever tripping it up."[20] Woollcott made an effort to revisit the production, but it only confirmed his original impressions that the abstract images were incongruous with the very real, humane performance of Lionel Barrymore on stage.[21] The *Nation* reported that the problem with Jones's design was that the "decorations are so meaningless, because so unrelated to reality, that all the pity of [Lady Macbeth's] distracted soul cannot shield our nerves from the assault of the boat-like hulks in the foreground."[22] Benjamin DeCasseres wrote, "When [Shakespeare] wrote 'castle' he did not mean a scenic tooth. . . . Art is art, and junk is junk, and never the twain shall meet—not in Shakespeare, at least."[23]

Only Jones's friend Kenneth Macgowan defended the design by writing, "I am convinced that *Macbeth* . . . is essentially an epoch-making production. . . . It is the beginning of something new."[24] However, he did believe that Jones "blundered" because he did not keep the overhead masks lowered throughout the play, which made the production "puzzling and inconclusive" to the audience. It was clear that the audience was not able to read the symbols embedded in the production design as an abstract expression of the fractured inner mind of the two main characters. Instead, the symbolic design seemed to draw focus from the honesty and simplicity of the text presented by actual actors on stage.

Jones could not fully understand or articulate, let alone stage, the impact of the unconscious on the art of theatre until he traveled to Zurich in 1926 to go into analysis with Carl Jung. It is not clear exactly why Jones decided to go to Switzerland. Dana Sue McDermott believes that it occurred at a time when Jones was frustrated with theatre and thinking about leaving the profession. She points out that he traveled to Zurich "almost immediately after his withdrawal from the Experimental Theatre, Inc." and that the thirty-nine-year-old Jones may have experienced a midlife crisis.[25] Jane T. Patterson, in "outing" Jones, speculates that the real reason he went to Zurich was that "[t]he psychic struggle between Jones's inner, homoerotic desires and the outer, social prohibitions against any form of transgressive sexuality that dominated his upbringing had reached a crucial impasse."[26] Axel Madsen supports this argument in *John Huston: A Biography,* in which he shares an antidote Huston once related about his aunt and uncle, Margaret Carrington and

Jones, whom he calls Bobby. Huston reportedly said, "Bobby was younger than Margaret, who continued to call herself Mrs. Carrington. Since he was a homosexual, she sent him to Vienna to see Sigmund Freud and later claimed the father of psychoanalysis had cured her husband."[27] While Huston had the location and psychoanalyst incorrect, the reason that Jones sought psychoanalytical help from the master Jung was likely related to both his dissatisfaction with the development of theatre and more personal issues.

While it may be unclear exactly *why* Jones went to Zurich, the influence of his work with Jung is clear. Jones ultimately concluded that

> Modern psychology has made us all familiar with the idea of the Unconscious. We have learned that beneath the surface of an ordinary, everyday, normal, casual conscious existence there lies a vast dynamic world of impulse and dream, a hinterland of energy which has an independent existence of its own and laws of its own: laws which motivate all our thoughts and our actions. This energy expresses itself to us in our conscious life in a never-ending stream of images, running incessantly through our minds from the cradle to the grave, and perhaps beyond. The concept of the Unconscious has profoundly influenced the intellectual life of our day. It has already become a commonplace of our thinking, and it is beginning to find an expression in our art.[28]

Jung likewise explained that "the unconscious produces a new idea of man . . . deified or divine, imprisoned, concealed, protected, usually dehumanized and expressed by abstract symbolism."[29] The psychologist also stated that symbols are produced "unconsciously and spontaneously, in the form of dreams."[30] He reasoned that anything we experience can also pass into our unconscious mind. Even though we may retain that experience in our conscious mind, it may also take on an unconscious element that can ultimately be recalled only through the analysis of our dreams. As McDermott explains, Jung used a method in therapy that "involved analyzing his patient's dreams through a process he called amplification. By this he meant enlarging the images or symbols present in a dream through mythological and archeological material as well as the patient's personal associations."[31] Jung believed that dreams are "the soil from which most symbols originally grow."[32] He noted that symbols are natural and spontaneous and that we cannot consciously create symbols. Given that symbols are products of the unconscious and that dreams allow us access to the unconscious, analysis of dreams connects our conscious thoughts to our unconscious mind, giving us a fuller understanding of ourselves.

It is easy to understand how these ideas could influence a man like Jones who spent his entire theatrical career struggling against the dominance of realism on the American stage. In *The Dramatic Imagination* he wrote, "Every play is a living dream: your dream, my dream—and that dream must not be blurred or darkened. The actors must be transparent to it. They may not exhibit. Their task is to reveal."[33] Jones wanted the theatre to stimulate the imagination and speak to the "eye of the mind." He believed that a scene design should not be a picture, but an "image," because, as Jung wrote, "the images produced in dreams are much more picturesque and vivid than the concepts and experiences that are their waking counterparts."[34]

Jones explained that the modern theatre should focus on the vivid, picturesque zone of dreams instead of presenting the conscious, waking reality that he termed the "camera minded." He advocated against realistic design choices "preoccupied with the sheer surface of things" because they signified that "insight dwindled into mere reporting. Our dreary averageness was publicized and glorified."[35] Instead of "camera minded" theatre, Jones believed that design should explore the world of dreams in order to connect our conscious and unconscious experiences.

Jones's designs always favored symbolic representation because he attempted to provide only what was necessary to convey the essential idea and atmosphere of the drama on stage. His scenery established a mood but the audience had to actively use their imaginations to complete the world in their own minds. This new approach earned him a reputation as a forward-thinking, progressive, and daringly original artist.

Film Experiments and Impressions

When John Hay "Jock" Whitney, a multi-millionaire sportsman, financier, art collector, diplomat, and occasional Broadway producer, bought a share of the new Technicolor corporation in 1933 and founded Pioneer Pictures, he asked Robert Edmond Jones to come to Hollywood as the film industry's first "color designer."[36] Jones experimented with Technicolor in the short film *La Cucaracha* and in a full-length film, *Becky Sharp.* As a production designer, he developed the costumes, settings, lighting, and color effects for both movies.

The 1935 film *Becky Sharp* was adapted from Langdon Mitchell's 1899 stage play and was loosely based on William Thackeray's novel *Vanity Fair.* Set during the Battle of Waterloo, the story focuses on Becky, a young girl from a low-class family, who befriends an upper-class girl named Amelia. Though Amelia's family grows to love Becky, the impetuous heroine still manages to ruin her life. The film illustrates Victorian class distinctions set neatly within the theatrical backdrop of extravagant empire gowns and military uniforms. The story provided an appropriately moral, yet decadently opulent context to introduce explosive color to the big screen. Ruth Woodbury Sedgwick reviewed the film and praised Jones with the following comment: "There is a shot of Miriam Hopkins, [as] Becky Sharp, in black and white, which fades into . . . color; the presentment of a living woman, with the heightened emphasis of fine painting. . . . [T]here [cannot] be any doubt that a good share of this beauty is due to Jones. He has put the designer's technique, his poet's vision at the service of this undisciplined infant."[37] However, not everyone shared Sedgwick's view. One critic commented that the cast looked like "boiled salmon dipped in mayonnaise,"[38] and *Time Magazine* reported that "the method of Color Director Robert Edmond Jones was to compose the chromatic values of each sequence as if it were a museum piece rather than an episode in a story."[39] In any case, Jones's contribution proved noteworthy at a time when mainstream critics did not routinely mention the contributions of designers.

Jones also designed and directed a ten-minute film of two scenes: one from *Hamlet,* featuring John Barrymore, and one starring Katharine Hepburn as Joan of Arc. In these color films, Jones manipulated film lighting to demonstrate his conviction that lighting must always paint the scene. He also experimented with a variety of ways to color the very white studio lights to effectively mirror the mood-enhancing qualities of more subtle, expressive theatre lighting. Clearly, Jones was not interested in reproducing a realistic world in his films. Instead, as Sedgwick pointed out in her review of *Becky Sharp,* he intended to theatrically use color "as a means of amplifying and enhancing dramatic action. [Color] can, he feels, heighten emotional effects just as music does, and perhaps even more legitimately."[40]

After Jones introduced theatre design techniques into his film work, he also wanted to introduce cinematic concepts into the theatre. In an article he wrote for the magazine *Vanity Fair,* he suggested that film created a certain "magic" for audiences that the theatre had lost. According to Jones, the theatre was historically a place of "enchantment" in which stars had a legendary aura about them. But now, Jones wrote, "The mystery is gone. Our theater has become scientific, objective, literal, analytic." He went on to explain that "[t]he well-knit dramas, the expert performances, the bright, brisk productions of today . . . cast no spell over us. We build no shrine to them in our memories." In contrast to "real people of flesh and blood," who acted on a stage, Jones noted that the actors on the screen are not real people, or "even real pictures." He wrote:

> The fact that they move and speak makes them something else. Translated through this new medium, they become, not pictures, but images. We see them, not objectively, as we might see the same actors in the theater, but subjectively, as Hamlet saw his father, in our mind's eye. These great beautiful images up there on the screen . . . whose perfect teeth loom over us, larger than the Radio City Tower, are not actual people at all. They are living symbols of beauty and power, living ideals, living idols. Unreal, intangible as they are, they have in some curious way the power to dominate and enthrall our imaginations as no flesh-and-blood actors could ever enthrall [us].[41]

Jones directly connected the intangible quality of film images to what he had learned about dreams from Carl Jung. Jones believed that motion pictures approach mythology and religion, where "our conscious critical faculties leave us. Reverence, curiosity, adoration crowd our minds. We just can't help worshiping the deities of the screen."[42] This echoes Jung's observation in his book *Psychology and Religion* that "numinous effect [leads to] the subsequent alteration of consciousness" and that religion "is the term that designates the attitude peculiar to a conscious which has been altered by the experience of the numinosum."[43] Jones doesn't want his theatrical design work to simply stimulate the imagination; he expects it to alter the viewer's consciousness. Jones articulates the deeper purpose of his work by stating, "it is for the poet to tell us why dreams are more potent than actualities, or whence comes the deep-seated craving in all of us to adore something outside of ourselves."[44] Jones displayed a sophisticated fascination for moving imagery and saw the potential of it in terms of enhancing live theatre performances. He saw film as a medium that could reflect both objective realism and mystic nonrealism in the same moment.

Of course, Piscator and Brecht had already used multimedia as a primary component of the epic theatre. In the 1930s the Federal Theatre Project had also attempted to translate this style onto the American stage with the "Living Newspaper Series" in America, and Tennessee Williams originally wanted to use projections in *The Glass Menagerie*. But most of these projects used primarily still projections or alternated moments of film with moments of stage action. Jones does not suggest using mere projected imagery; he encouraged a full integration and simultaneous use of motion pictures and stage action. He also did not echo Brecht's idea of alienation. Rather, he subscribed to Max Reinhardt's goal of drawing people into the theatre production on a deeply subconscious and emotional level. As Jones put it, "In life, as we live it, our inner experience runs parallel to our outer experience but seldom meets it. The two varieties of experience are rarely fused. But the new drama will present to us not only our life in relation to the world we live in but our relation to our own inner dream. Here is its promise. Seeing it; hearing it; experiencing it; we can become whole once more."[45]

Jung similarly wrote "that even when our senses react to real phenomena . . . they are somehow translated from the realm of reality into that of the mind."[46] Jones believed in the importance of expressing both the realm of the conscious and the unconscious on stage because, like Jung, Jones believed that a dependence on objective realism ultimately would separate individuals from their collective souls. According to Jung, "our present lives are dominated by the goddess Reason, who is our greatest and most tragic illusion. By the aid of reason, so we assure ourselves, we have 'conquered' nature."[47] Instead, Jung urges us to explore our true natures by revealing, processing, and coming to terms with both our conscious and unconscious desires through the exploration of dreams. Jones evidently believes that staging symbolic "poetic idealism" is also a viable avenue for this important work.

Jones and Hopkins first tried to stage the connection between man's inner and outer experiences in their 1921 production of *Macbeth*. The use of the three masks as symbols of our "unconscious devils" illustrates Jones's desire to explore the essence of the subconscious on stage. The rejection of this production led him to retreat from providing overtly subconscious symbols on stage, and he eventually turned to film as a means to continue this abstract experimentation. Psychotherapy with Carl Jung gave Jones a better understanding of the function of symbols and the connection of the subconscious and conscious selves. His film experience opened up a new world of possibilities. He ultimately saw film as a medium that leads us easily into unconscious experience, whereas the theatre seemed stuck in a conscious frame. He came to believe that the seamless integration of film and theatre would be the best way to integrate both the conscious and subconscious. He wanted the moving film to highlight the actor on stage and create a landscape that all audience members could interpret within the mystic and realistic frames of the play. Ideally the film would not dwarf the actor on stage or distract audiences; rather it would complete the picture. As we know, numerous contemporary designers and directors are now beginning to explore ways to realize Jones's 1940s dream of the theatre of the future. Nevertheless he never had the chance to initiate these types of integrated projects himself.

By examining the working practices of the Broadway theatre during

Jones's career and his own work in the film industry, we get a good sense of why it was difficult, if not impossible, to experiment with this proposed new style of media integration. Then, as now, mainstream commercial interests often prompt investors to support artistic projects that do not demand audiences to think very far beyond the objective images on the screen and stage. Clearly many of the critics who viewed Jones's ill-fated production of *Macbeth* failed to make the psychological and/or intellectual leap to view the setting as a symbolic representation of the main character's inner life.

Delving into the subconscious is difficult, time-consuming, and potentially frustrating work. In general, audiences prefer to pay for relaxing, "camera minded" entertainment that allows us to escape the exhaustion and anxiety of our lived lives. Jones's idea for the theatre of the future seemed predicated on the fact that society would evolve to a point at which the unification of the external and the unconscious worlds would be much more mainstream.

Jones's seminal work, *The Dramatic Imagination,* has inspired generations of theatre practitioners. It is easy to look at the combined essays as merely a well-written guide to the practical art of theatre making. Nevertheless, it is also valuable to read it in relation to Jones's larger body of work. It is clear that he saw theatre as more than just a technical profession and a form of artistic entertainment. His philosophical vision extended far beyond the stage. He hoped the theatre of the future would allow audiences to view the stage picture as a vital avenue for important psychic therapy that would inspire us to explore messages buried within our unconscious mind's eye.

Notes

1. Brooks Atkinson, "Standard Jones, Designer: Notes on the Case of Robert Edmond Jones, the Scene Designer Who Keeps His Own Faith Through the Years," *New York Times,* June 22, 1941, X1.

2. Robert Edmond Jones, "The Theatre of the Future," in *Towards a New Theatre: The Lectures of Robert Edmond Jones,* ed. Delbert Unruh (New York: Limelight Editions, 1992), 31–32.

3. Kenneth Macgowan, "Robert Edmond Jones: A Tribute," *Educational Theatre Journal* 7, no. 2 (May 1955): 136.

4. Mabel Dodge Luhan, *Movers and Shakers* (Albuquerque: University of New Mexico Press, 1985), 204.

5. Robert Edmond Jones, letter to Kenneth Macgowan, n.d., Special Collections, Research Library, University of California, Los Angeles.

6. Luhan, *Movers and Shakers,* 214.

7. Heinrich Huesmann, *Welttheater Reinhardt: Bauten, Spielstatten, Inszenierungen* (Munich: Prestel-Verlag, 1983), 513–24.

8. J. L. Styan, *Max Reinhardt* (Cambridge: Cambridge University Press, 1982), 52.

9. Robert Edmond Jones, "The Future Decorative Art of the Theatre," in *Scene Design for Stage and Screen,* ed. Orville K. Larson (East Lansing: Michigan State University Press, 1961), 13.

10. Kenneth Macgowan, "The New Path of the Theatre," *Theatre Arts Magazine* 1 (April 1919): 84–86.

11. Dana Sue McDermott, "Creativity in the Theatre: Robert Edmond Jones and C. G. Jung," *Theatre Journal* 36, no. 2 (May 1984): 214.

12. C. P. Orberndorf, "The Literary and Historical Contributions of Dr. Smith-Ely Jelliffe," *Journal of Nervous and Mental Disease* 106, no. 3 (September 1947): 228–32.

13. Robert Edmond Jones, *Drawings for the Theatre,* ed. Donald Oenslager (1925; repr., New York: Theatre Arts Books, 1970), 16.

14. Arthur Hopkins, "The Approaching 'Macbeth,'" *New York Times,* February 6, 1921, X1.

15. Arthur Hopkins, *To a Lonely Boy* (Garden City, NY: Doubleday, Doran, 1937), 224.

16. Alexander Woollcott, review of *Macbeth,* by William Shakespeare, directed by Arthur Hopkins, Apollo Theatre, New York, *New York Times,* February 18, 1921, 20.

17. Ibid.

18. Carl Gustav Jung, "Approaching the Unconscious," in *Man and His Symbols,* ed. Carl G. Jung and M. L. von Franz (Garden City, NY: Doubleday, 1964), 20.

19. Woollcott, review of *Macbeth,* 20.

20. Alexander Woollcott, "Second Thoughts on First Nights," *New York Times,* February 20, 1921, X1.

21. Ibid.

22. "*Macbeth* in the Void," *Nation* 112 (March 2, 1921): 350.

23. Benjamin DeCasseres, "A Drift in the Roaring Forties," *Theatre Magazine* 36, no. 5 (November 1922): 306.

24. Kenneth Macgowan, "The Centre of the Stage," *Theatre Arts Magazine* 5, no. 2 (April 1921): 92.

25. McDermott, "Creativity in the Theatre," 213, 216.

26. Jane T. Patterson, "Not as Other Boys: Robert Edmond Jones and Designs of Desire," in *Staging Desire: Queer Readings of American Theater History,* ed. Kim Marra and Robert A. Schanke (Ann Arbor: University of Michigan Press, 2006), 347–48.

27. Axel Madsen, *John Huston: A Biography* (Garden City, NY: Doubleday, 1978), 20–21.

28. Robert Edmond Jones, *The Dramatic Imagination* (New York: Routledge, 2004), 15–16.

29. Carl Gustav Jung, *Psychology and Religion* (New Haven, CT: Yale University Press, 1938), 106.

30. Jung, "Approaching the Unconscious," 21.
31. McDermott, "Creativity in the Theatre," 215.
32. Jung, "Approaching the Unconscious," 39.
33. Jones, *Dramatic Imagination,* 28.
34. Jung, "Approaching the Unconscious," 43.
35. Jones, *Towards a New Theatre,* 22.
36. Ruth Woodbury Sedgwick, "Colorist," *Stage* 12, no. 10 (July 1935): 37.
37. Ibid.
38. Internet Movie Database, "Trivia for Becky Sharp," http://www.imdb.com/title/tt0026104/trivia.
39. "The New Pictures," *Time Magazine,* March 2, 1936, http://www.time.com (accessed May 20, 2008).
40. Sedgwick, "Colorist," 37.
41. Robert Edmond Jones, "My Hollywood," *Vanity Fair,* October 1934, 37.
42. Ibid.
43. Jung, *Psychology and Religion,* 6.
44. Jones, "My Hollywood," 37.
45. Jones, *Towards a New Theatre,* 34.
46. Jung, "Approaching the Unconscious," 23.
47. Ibid., 101.

Frank Castorf at the Volksbühne am Rosa Luxembourg Platz

Alienation Techniques and the Use of Mediated Material on the Live Stage

Steve Earnest

THROUGHOUT THE latter years of the twentieth century and into the twenty-first century, the use of film, video, and mediated settings became an increasingly important aspect of scenography at Germany's largest state theatres. Key developments in stage technology—such as the use of high-powered projectors, the use of glass slides instead of those made of plastic or acetate, and the increasing use of digital video technologies—permitted greater experimentation with live and mediated action and comprised a permanent part of the German theatre landscape. Given the immense technical capabilities of the German state theatres in addition to their high levels of national funding, multimedia advances have been arguably more profound in Germany than in any place in the world. Perhaps no stage director was more influential in this arena than Frank Castorf, noted *Intendant* of Berlin's Volksbühne am Rosa Luxembourg Platz. From the mid-1980s until the first decade of the twenty-first century Castorf integrated the arts of theatre and cinema in a manner that both heightened the art of stage direction in Germany as well as modified and advanced numerous theatrical concepts, such as the Brechtian concept of *verfremdungseffekt,* or alienation. Other ideas associated with Brechtian epic theatre, such as montage and the use of music, as well as more radical techniques of deconstruction and postmodern structure as advanced by Heiner Müller, were also employed by Castorf. Unique in his combination of the dual aesthetic of theatre and film, Castorf's use of cameras on the live stage has challenged theatre aesthetics by contrasting the live stage figure with the full or partial human face in close-up, by utilizing multiple cameras on different areas of the theatrical space and by incorporating the act of filming and camera work into the action of his works. Three of Castorf's productions, Fyodor Dostoyevsky's *Erniedrigte Und Beleidigte* (*The Insulted and the Injured*), Mikhail Bulgakov's *The Master and Margarita,* and Bertolt Brecht's *Der Jasager/Der Neinsager* (*He Who Says Yes/He Who Says No*),[1] serve to illustrate Castorf's varied directorial approaches and his unique film/theatre aesthetic.

Founded in 1914, the Volksbühne has historically been a regular site for live productions that experimented with multimedia and film. The early period of the Volksbühne included multimedia work by Erwin Piscator and the young Brecht; its middle period as a state theatre of the German Democratic Republic (GDR) featured radical experimentation involving Soviet-influenced film and video techniques under the leadership of Benno Besson. Throughout the later years of the GDR and into the post-reunification period, Castorf emerged into the Berlin scene as an *enfant terrible,* a radical young director who mounted numerous shockingly provocative productions that challenged GDR politics while pushing artistic mores to their breaking point and that subsequently advanced postmodern techniques such as collage structure and deconstruction. An important element of Castorf's dramaturgy and theatre aesthetic at the Volksbühne was the commingling of live and mediated material as well as the inclusion of rock music (the Rolling Stones and other iconic rock groups have always been prevalent in his work) and numerous references to popular culture. Having served as *Intendant* since 1992, Castorf steadily developed a reputation as one of the most provocative, innovative, yet notorious directors on the German stage. As a student of Theaterwissenschaft (or Theatre Science) at Humbolt Universität in Berlin in the 1970s, Castorf had studied the theories of Brecht but favored the more radical structure of Müller in practice. Because the strict stance regarding socialist realism had become more relaxed in the GDR in the 1970s, Müller's synthetic fragments and collage works (such as *Hamletmaschine,* published in 1971) had become extremely influential among academics. After staging a number of television projects for the East German Television system (DEFA) Castorf began to incorporate ideas of collage structure, including video and other mediated material, into his directorial vision. Alternatively praised and demonized by critics and theatre personnel alike, Castorf has been labeled a "text destroyer," often leaving very little of a work's original text intact.[2] Additionally he has been equally celebrated and criticized for imbuing productions at the Volksbühne with shocking images and stage activities, numerous mediated approaches, and virtual obliteration of theatre texts in favor of combining and contrasting literature with popular culture, current events, and political propaganda. His first experiment with a live camera on stage came in 1987 in a production of Ibsen's *The Enemy of the People;* it was then that he began experimenting with one of the major visual themes of his work—the relationship between theatrical space and camera close-ups. This technique, widely used on the world stage in the twenty-first century, was advanced by Castorf in collaboration with videographer Jan Speckenbach and his frequent scenic design partner Bert Neumann. Another technique pioneered by Castorf was the use of embedded cameras within the theatrical environment in order to present stage perspectives not seen directly by the audience. This revolutionary approach, virtually unused on the stage prior to Castorf's implementation, characterized numerous later Castorf productions. Considering the many directors in the twenty-first century that have embraced multimedia direction—such as Christoph Schlingensief, Peter Sellars, Robert LePage, and Katie Mitchell—Castorf's early development of these various techniques along with his radical approaches to textual deconstruction gave rise to the term *Regietheater,* a movement centered in Germany but which proliferated across Europe and to the United States. Numerous radical directorial approaches emerged in the late twentieth century and, at least for a time, none were more shocking and radical than that of Castorf at the Volksbühne.[3]

The first full-fledged multimedia production by Castorf was *Cocaine* (1991), a work written and developed by Castorf that featured cameras placed throughout the theatrical setting, revealing areas not visible to the audience, with material projected onto screens allowing the audience to witness moments that would normally be hidden from them. While little information is available about this work—it was staged in the East German provincial theatre of Anklam—Castorf began to use this technique throughout his career as a conscious choice to contrast the seen realities of the stage environment with hidden realities that drive and supplement the visible stage environments. While this staging element was not specifically discussed by Brecht in his theories regarding alienation, one might argue that, in the same way that slide projections and other scenic material either reinforced or contradicted the stage action, Castorf's inclusion of live-time video sequences have advanced techniques stated by Brecht. In his essay "The German Drama: Pre-Hitler" Brecht notes: "Piscator, who without a doubt is one of the most important theatre men of all times, began to transform its scenic potentialities. He introduced a number of far-reaching innovations. One of them was his use of film and of film projections as an integral part of the settings. The setting was thus awakened to life and began to play on its own, so to speak; the film was a new, gigantic actor that helped to narrate events.

By means of it documents could be shown as part of the scenic background, figures and statistics. Simultaneous events in different places could be seen together."[4]

While this quote documents the innovations of Piscator as opposed to Brecht, it was Brecht who articulated their use and the importance of these techniques in the new, epic theatre he proposed. Brecht was highly influenced by these techniques (which were, coincidentally, first implemented at the Volksbühne) and more clearly than anyone stated their importance in his published writings. While Brecht's actual use of these techniques may have been less prolific than that of Piscator, his analysis and observation of these elements have been far more important than any other pre-1950 writing about this approach.[5]

Since his appointment as *Intendant* at the Volksbühne in 1992, Castorf began a number of trends that would both solidify the Volksbühne's place as one of Germany's great theatres of the modern age as well as elevate it as one of the theatre world's great sites for experimentation in the realm of avant-garde work. Castorf began by hiring numerous young innovative directors, like Andreas Kriegenburg, René Pollesch, and Christoph Marthaler and, given the immense financial resources of the Volksbühne, offering them an unparalleled environment for the creation of new radical works. Second, he employed a radically different company of actors, many of whom had been considered problem actors due to their strong political leanings or approaches to rehearsal and performance and who had been released from other state theatres. Finally, Castorf began to greatly diversify the repertory and, unlike the bulk of German state theatres, which generally presented German and world classics interspersed with new and original works, featured nontraditional pieces and "deconstructed" works as the majority of its offerings. One aspect of Castorf's choice of repertory included a shift to the staging of literary novels as opposed to plays or works written specifically for theatrical production. According to Castorf, "Novels possess a complexity that I do not find in plays and the structure of novels corresponds more accurately with the political realities and complexities of our time. A play possesses a hermetic quality leading one to think that the world is okay the way it is. For me the complexity, the chaos, the diversity and the many possibilities to narrate a story are all in the novel."[6]

One of Castorf's most important stagings of literary works was Dostoyevsky's *The Insulted and the Injured,* presented at the Volksbühne in 2000 and selected for participation at the 2001 Berliner Theatertreffen, a festival featuring the ten best German-language productions of a given theatrical season. Castorf's work was featured at the yearly festival

Thoughts of the young woman (Katrin Angerer) entice the writer, played by Martin Wuttke in Castorf's *The Insulted and the Injured* at Berlin's Volksbühne, on tour at UCLA. Copyright © 2001 Thomas Aurin.

no less than eight times from 1993 to 2002, more than any other German director of that period. Dostoyevsky wrote *The Insulted and the Injured* as a serialized novel primarily as a way to make money during difficult times. The text appealed to Castorf because of its status as a "big city novel" with abundance of "economic and erotic content."[7] Given Castorf's desire to include references to popular culture in his works, he also drew upon the popularity of the reality television series in the twenty-first century. He felt that *The Insulted and the Injured* contained many unknown, "hidden," or "concealed" aspects that relied on chance (at least in the context of the novel) and begged comparison with reality television shows like *Big Brother* that relied on structural devices such as contradictory live action/video segments and displayed characters living their daily lives with interruptions and influences from an outside source. Carl Hegemann, dramaturg for *The Insulted and the Injured,* noted that, according to Castorf, one of the prevailing themes of the work was the motto "he who doesn't conspicuously compete or participate gains a business advantage," an allusion to the role of the writer (noted later) who often stands outside the action and comments on it.[8] Bert Neumann's setting for the nearly five-hour work consisted of an onstage dwelling—

a fully developed two-level housing unit whose interior was completely concealed from the audience's view by the outer walls. According to Castorf, this technique broke with the long-standing theatrical convention that everything on stage should be seen.[9] The interior action scenes were revealed via an elaborate system of internal cameras placed throughout the flat, with the live-time video revealed on three separate screens—one above and one on each side of the flat. Jan Speckenbach's elaborate system of cameras allowed numerous patterns of action to take place throughout the work. First, it enabled the audience to see interior scenes that were completely hidden by the exterior walls of the unit. Second, it allowed for scenes of contradiction to be played as characters stood outside the dwelling saying one thing, while the action inside the dwelling displayed the opposite. For example, the deranged, dying orphan girl adopted by the writer Vanya (played by Martin Wuttke, regular Volksbühne actor and international star) turned out to be a subversive sex kitten, and many sex scenes were played inside while Vanya stood outside thinking aloud, smoking, or playing scenes with other characters. Finally, it permitted Castorf to develop a fantasy site where characters deepest dreams and obsessions could be revealed on the screen as a quasi "mental landscape." Numerous pre-taped fantastical scenes involving the characters, including scenes of sexuality that bordered on pornography, were presented.

According to Hegemann, the camera, as used by Castorf, represents the last and greatest means of artistic distancing; the camera can present an individual or group of individuals and can simultaneously show something particular about the individual and something general or archetypal about humanity as well. A hypothetical example cited by Hegemann was that of the angry crowd shouting at a political candidate or at a group of policemen and the action and events that evolved. After the wide shot of the angry mob and its sheer volume and power, camera close-ups can reveal individuals saying very relevant solo lines, a mother holding a baby, tears streaming down faces, and other extremely individual moments. The camera allows for the possibility of displaying humanity in ways that people would like to be seen as well as in ways that they do not want to be seen.[10] Hegemann noted that these juxtapositions extended Brecht's ideas in ways that were not commonly used when his theories were written. Therefore the concept of Brechtian alienation, as used by Castorf, includes elements of both expressionism and postmodernism; the audience's perception and interaction with the stage narrative are distanced via mental landscapes produced by video, contemporary interpolations, references to outside events, and outright camp. The awareness of the live-time film process draws attention to the mak-

Volksbühne actors Henry Hubchen, Irina Potapenko, and Bernhard Schützin in *The Insulted and the Injured* at UCLA. Copyright © 2001 Thomas Aurin.

ing of the work as referenced by Brecht in several of his writings.[11] Using Brecht's ideas of alienation as a starting point, Castorf's extensions and adaptations of Brecht's theories have yielded a slightly different version of alienation, but nevertheless numerous techniques that attempt to critically distance the viewers from the action.

In both *The Insulted and the Injured* as well as in *He Who Says Yes/He Who Says No,* Castorf incorporated references to typical capitalist marketing techniques such as videotaped and still images that were enticing, arousing, alluring, and unavoidable. Hegemann noted that Castorf wanted to show that in contemporary society—particularly in the United States—there is a trend in the media that emphasizes material possessions as opposed to the "actual act of just living or being."[12] According to Hegemann this was particularly apparent in 1980s American television series like *Dallas* that continually stressed materialism and the coveting of material possessions and property. Hegemann also noted that American television series were populated by stock characters and situations that were so overused that one could take the situations and view them indirectly (that is, interpolate them into an existing scene or include a video clip within the context of a scene) in order to reconsider their meaning in contrast to a live-time situation of a scene in a play with which they were being considered. He emphasized that the real value of their inclusion as scenes of alienation required that they be shown in contrast with related, live material.[13]

Utilizing a similar approach, Castorf's *The Master and Margarita* premiered at the Volksbühne later in 2001. In Bulgakov's satire, the Devil arrives in Stalinist Moscow in the 1930s and creates confusion and havoc throughout society as the unreal becomes reality and reality turns into fiction. The story operates on multiple levels; a narrator compares Stalin's reign of terror with the crucifixion of Christ as the real devil meets a "Christ figure" (a Moscow businessman) against the backdrop of the chaotic bureaucracy of Stalin's regime. Again Bert Neumann's setting included an extensive set of internal cameras, with even more of the stage space hidden from audience view than with the Dostoyevsky work. Situated behind the interior dwelling occupied by the "Jesus" character was a series of internal spaces—an asylum consisting of a cell, a shower, and a bathhouse; a film set; and a model of Moscow. The nature of this work was more like reality television than his previous efforts as the video recording was nonstop, provided by the internal cameras and by a tracking camera that moved around the space in 360 degrees. The permeating images of "Big Brother" metaphorically alluded to ideas of state control and the permanent loss of private life that individuals undergo when living under surveillance. In this work, more than in any other of Castorf's previous efforts, the margin between live stage action and mediated sequences was blurred to the point that it was difficult to distinguish between them, as characters were shown in pre-taped sequences that blended perfectly with the stage action.[14]

Castorf's 2007 production of Brecht's *Der Jasager/Der Neinsager* (still in the repertory at the Volksbühne in 2010) uniquely illustrated the process whereby the live actor was captured on film via the live performance. While *The Insulted and the Injured* and *The Master and Margarita* experimented with the presentation and selection of masked or hidden onstage actions that were revealed only via videotaped scenes—many of them in close-up—during live stage action, *He Who Says Yes/He Who Says No* used an onstage camera crew to set up and capture each of the scenes in an attempt to present multiple perspectives of the action to the audience. Given his interest in Brechtian production styles, Castorf extended Brechtian techniques of distancing and alienation in this production by using video techniques to compare the live stage action with the action captured onstage through video technology.

Staged in the enormous Grosse Bühne, the largest of the Volksbühne's three theatre spaces, audience members were led by Volksbühne staff through the auditorium and into the backstage area where they were seated in the stage-left offstage area facing the stage, which had been lowered from its normal height to a position about twelve feet below the typical stage surface. The setting was the exterior of a cabaret, the "Salon Gier," with the words "Dreams for Sale" inscribed on the marquee. *He Who Says Yes/He Who Says No* was staged in cabaret format as two actresses, Anna Kratky and Ruth Rosenfeld, served as the chorus, singing the opening sequences in a campy, comedic "lounge lizard" style accompanied by their maestro, Bernhard Schütz, on piano. Castorf's multimedia approach included a camera operator and assistant who moved throughout the environment, capturing the action via live-time video. Each scene was blocked and realized from both a stage as well as a film standpoint—the blocking of the camera operator was equally important to that of the on-stage action. The captured scenes were projected onto a screen situated above the cabaret exterior, expanding the work's scale as multiple perspectives, reactions, and ironic commentary of the chorus were revealed in live-time video projection. Brigitte Cuvelier, Maximilian Speck, and Axel Wandtke performed the roles of the student, mother, and teacher, gradually emerging into the preestablished cabaret setting and telling the story of the journey into the mountains and the agreement to accept suicide in order to sustain the movement's progress. *He Who Says Yes/He Who Says No* was actually a combination of the two short operas *Der Jasager* and *Der Neinsager;* Castorf included the second work as a comic decision by the film crew to restage the ending after the student refused to jump off the mountain instead of agreeing to do it. Alienation was achieved in the piece via two viewpoints or "lenses": from the standpoint of presenting the work as a live theatrical event and from the standpoint of showing the audience multiple perspectives within the work as it was captured by a camera. The actors utilized three basic performance styles—realism, distanced "reporting," and ironic commentary. The student played his role, including the decisions that he was forced to make, in a realistic manner, considering the situations he faced (for instance, waiting for camera shots to be set up). The chorus, on the other hand, played to the camera, posed mockingly, and adopted something of a crooning delivery style, often breaking into hysterical laughter as a reaction to the stage events followed by a "freeze" to incite comic effect. The mother and teacher, however, lived somewhere between the realistic world of the student and the overtly presentational world of the chorus. Both characters used the camera to ironically contradict what was transpiring on stage as well as what they were actually saying at times. For example, during the final moments of the play, the teacher asks the boy, who has fallen ill, whether or not he will turn back so that the "expedition" could continue. The dialogue is as follows:

> THE TEACHER: Custom ordains that he who has fallen ill should answer: You should not turn back.
> THE BOY: I understand.
> THE TEACHER: Do you ask us to turn back on your account?
> THE BOY: You should not turn back!
> THE TEACHER: Then you consent to being left behind?
> THE BOY: I will think about it. *Pause for reflection.* Yes, I consent.
> THE TEACHER: He has answered in accordance with necessity.[15]

After having consented that the "expedition" will continue without him, the boy then consents to being hurled into the valley so that his death will be immediate and he will not have to die alone. The straightforwardness of the above dialogue was captured in extreme camera close-up, and ironic glances and facial commentary reflected the underlying truth and hidden reality that the young boy was essentially agreeing to give up his life for the expedition. Realistic tears in the boy's face contrasted with stern, pressuring looks by the teacher revealed that, in truth, the boy had no choice and that he was forced to relinquish his life so that the expedition (or Communism) could move forward. This ironic juxtaposition between the stated text and the intention of the characters represents another level of the epic quality of Castorf's directorial vision.

Castorf's approach—including his use of montage, video and film, rock music, and the masking of hidden stage realities—combines certain elements of postmodernism and expressionism and also expands Brecht's concept of alienation. By hiding large portions of the stage environment from the audience and revealing hidden areas at designated times only via mediated sources, Castorf controls the audience's perception of the stage narrative via the mixture of live action and media. Structurally, these devices serve to interrupt the stage action and distance the audience from the happenings in the world of the play. Second, Castorf's work contrasts live actors with mediated images, often in drastic scale to one another. This forces the audience to step outside the normal boundaries of either live or mediated performance and consider the two performance styles simultaneously. Alienation is achieved in Castorf's works through the inclusion of the filming process as part of the work's mise-en-scène. This awareness and display of the process was a key element in Brecht's epic production approach; Castorf's productions consistently draw attention to and comment on the process of what is taking place on the stage. Finally, Castorf believes that the most important element

In a scene from *Der Jasager/Der Neinsager*, Axel Wandtke watches as the teacher (Bernhard Schütz) offers water to the mother (Brigitte Cuvelier), all captured on camera by Andreas Dienert. Copyright © 2008 Thomas Aurin.

of the camera is that it shapes and literally "creates" reality. For example, in his production of *Forever Young*, an adaptation of Tennessee Williams's *Sweet Bird of Youth* (not specifically analyzed in this essay), Princess Kosmonopolis tells Chance Wayne that she refuses to have her feet filmed in a scene once because they are too ugly. Wayne then asks her, "Then why not use a foot double?" During the course of their dialogue a videotaped scene shows the princess's actual "ugly" feet being captured on video and then being replaced by a prettier set of feet. Castorf uses this example to prove the fact that film has the power to construct new realities that supersede other realities of the stage, and that the created new realities can essentially replace realism.

Hegemann notes that in Castorf's work, "a hybrid style of performance is created that cannot be achieved by either film or theatre alone."[16] The unique combination of live and mediated action has fundamentally changed many of the conditions that were basically the same for over two thousand years. Ideas such as including space on the stage that is not visible to the audience but that is revealed through mediated sources, dark areas presented to the audience via infrared camera lenses, and prerecorded mediated action that delves into the inner, psychological lives of the characters fundamentally altered many principles of the live stage that traditionally consisted of happenings on a "viewing place" where everything was seen by all. While all elements of the stage narrative are still seen in Castorf's work, much of the material that is viewed has been prerecorded and removed from the live stage. The camera gives the actors yet another means with which to interact with the audience—many times in Castorf productions the actors find moments in the context of the scene to look directly into the camera, but not so much into the camera itself as into the faces of the audience members directly. This dual interaction with the audience, magnified via the lens of the camera yet realized in a live environment, intensifies the actors' connection with the audience.[17]

While not always popular with critics or even audience members, Castorf's theatrical productions have challenged existing performance standards throughout Europe and have separated productions at the Volksbühne from the rest of the German-speaking world. Though not all of his works involve video and mediated material, Castorf's theatrical vision has both riddled and rocked European theatre critics, who have noted that Castorf's works have "broken all the rules, so who can say what comes next" and that he has "brow beaten his audiences to the point of submission."[18] More positive reviews have noted that Castorf's works are "stimulating and innovative" as well as "appropriate to the current world in their combination of mediated as well as live text."[19] While it is clear that Castorf is not the only major world figure to experiment in the merger of film and theatre, it is certain that, given his ample resources as well as his commitment to the advancement of the mixture of live and mediated material, Castorf's works are among the most highly developed examples of a hybrid film/theatre genre.

Notes

1. Brecht's two companion *Lehrstücke* were staged as a single work by Castorf in 2007 at the Volksbühne am Rosa Luxembourg Platz.

2. Sally McGrane, "Outrageousness, Herr Director, Is a Tough Act to Follow," *New York Times,* January 14, 2007.

3. Marvin Carlson, "Frank Castorf and the Volksbühne: Berlin's Theatre of Deconstruction," in *Contemporary European Theatre Directors,* ed. Maria Delgado and Dan Rebellato (New York: Routledge Press, 2010).

4. Bertolt Brecht, "The German Drama: Pre-Hitler," in *Brecht on Theatre,* ed. John Willett (New York: Hill and Wang, 1992), 77–78.

5. During the latter stages of Brecht's career, when he could have been experimenting with multimedia in performance, he was severely restricted by the policies of socialist realism in the GDR.

6. Frank Castorf, "Not Realism but Reality," *Encore Magazine: A Publication of UCLA Live,* December 2003, 56.

7. Ibid.

8. Ibid.

9. Ibid.

10. Carl Hegemann, "Program Notes: *Erniedrigte Und Beleidigte,*" *Encore Magazine: A Publication of UCLA Live,* December 2003, 55.

11. Brecht alludes to these techniques in numerous writings but specifically in "On Experimental Theatre" (1959) and "Theatre for Pleasure or Theatre for Instruction" (1957).

12. Hegemann, "Program Notes," 55.

13. Ibid.

14. Yvonne Spielmann, "Theater Goes Reality TV: *The Master and Margarita* at the Volksbühne in Berlin, Germany," Leonardo Online Reviews, MIT Press, December 2002, http://lmj.mit.edu/reviews/dec2002/REALITY_spielmann.html.

15. Bertolt Brecht, *The Measures Taken and Other Lehrstücke* (London: Methuen Drama, 1977).

16. Carl Hegemann, "Was bewirkt die Kamera auf der Bühne bei den Schauspielen?" *Dramaturg* (January 2004).

17. Ivan Hagendoorn, "Portrait: Frank Castorf," Goethe-Institut, http://www.goethe.de/kue/the/reg/reg/as/cas.

18. McGrane, "Outrageousness, Herr Director."

19. Hegemann, "Program Notes," 56.

The London Theatre Goes Digital

Divergent Responses to the New Media

Leslie A. Wade

IN A 2001 *New Theatre Quarterly* essay, Baz Kershaw highlights a concern with the receding status of the British theatre, a condition he describes as "theatre at the end of its tether."[1] For Kershaw, theatre in Britain had come to a point of jeopardy, with a diminished role in cultural conversation, a stagnation in artistic experimentation, and a self-conscious awareness that many viewed its current forms and practices as out of touch, even quaint. His essay recounts the dismay of many theatre directors and producers, who expressed worry over the theatre's waning confidence and sense of adventure, its failure to address and respond to actual social needs. In assessing the growing suspicion that British theatre was losing its relevance and power of engagement, Kershaw identifies the cultural shift from analog to digital as a primary contributor to this experience of crisis—and the cause of trepidation for many theatre artists. London arts leader Michael Kustow, in fact, called for theatre to bolster its defenses, urging extreme caution in view of digital encroachment: "Theatre may be undergoing life-threatening mutations. . . . I am therefore warning against . . . theatre subsumed by webs and networks."[2]

Kershaw's analysis effectively addresses the apprehensive state of British theatre and its unease regarding a digital future. This essay extends such investigation and documents how new media technologies have proliferated since Kershaw's writing. This essay also situates the theatre's lingering media anxiety within a broader context, that of a nation under duress, of global market forces, of multiple communities seeking coexistence without coercion. In short, digital capabilities have brought theatre to a kind of reckoning—how to best negotiate the future of traditional stage practice in the face of twenty-first-century stage modalities. The digital turn furthermore implicates theatre in a discussion of the human and post-human. What is at stake is not just the priority of a stage practice or performance form but vying conceptions of human interconnection (which may invoke spiritual dimensions). That the London theatre remains ambivalent in its embrace of mediatization—evidenced in this essay's discussion of two recent productions, *Time and the Conways* and *Jerusalem*—indicates not just a continued concern with the digital's colonization of the live theatre event, but with the stage's complicity in limiting or expanding possible definitions of the human. British theatre of the early twenty-first century has consequently exhibited both panic and exuberance, challenged to reimagine its understanding of both art and responsibility.

If Kershaw's essay points to the 1990s' explosion of digital performance and its feared intrusion upon the theatre, the year 2009 stands as a historical marker, a time when new media technology confirmed its legitimacy and won full partnership in British theatre operations. At this juncture one can claim without question that British theatre had become mediatized (mediatization here includes satellite simulcasts, digital recordings, online downloads, as well as digital media effects employed within stage performances). Despite Kustow's warnings, and the prior panic in the theatre community, the theatre embraced and partnered with the digital media in ways that only years before could not have been imagined.

The year 2009 witnessed an astonishing number of new ventures that are bringing British theatre into global digital networks, ventures that challenge not only the conception of audience and product delivery but the definition of theatre itself. The summer saw the first installment of the National Theatre's Live project, a simulcast of its highly acclaimed production of *Phèdre,* starring Helen Mirren and Dominic Cooper. The staging was aired live in Britain and more than sixteen other countries, including the United States, Australia, New Zealand, and Malta. Heralded as a grand success, the broadcast appeared in over 270 cinemas before an estimated 50,000 viewers.[3] The Live project has gone on to simulcast *All's Well That Ends Well* and Marc Ravenhill's adaptation of *Nation.* That year also marked the launch of the Greenwich Theatre's Stage on Screen project, which created DVDs of its *Doctor Faustus* and *The School for Scandal* productions for distribution through school systems. The Globe as well entered into the digital market, announcing that it would screen productions to a global audience as part of a new partnership with Opus Arte, a production company owned by the Royal Opera House. Recordings of the 2009 season productions of *Romeo and Juliet, Love's Labour's Lost,* and *As You Like It* will be shown in around eighty cinema screens in Britain and in over five hundred worldwide,[4] though the performances will not be broadcast live, as with the National Theatre. Such efforts are bringing new technologies into novel relationships with stage production and creating entertainment products that can be sold worldwide, expanding the repute and profitability of the British theatre. These initiatives promise to attract new audiences and to position theatre presentation as a vital component in the emerging complex of digital commodity.

Perhaps the most discussed of these ventures, however, has been the launching of the Digital Theatre project, the brainchild of Robert Delamere and Tom Shaw, who have raised over a million pounds for the effort's start-up. Digital Theatre has partnered with the Royal Shakespeare Company, the Royal Court Theatre, the Almeida Theatre Company, the English Touring Theatre, and the Young Vic, which have consented to offer their works for sale on the Web.[5] Digital Theatre, in short, records the live plays and sells them (after the run of the show has concluded) to customers as a downloadable file—the procedure parallels the marketing of new music by iTunes. In this format plays transform into iPod downloads. A single play can be accessed for around nine British pounds. The Digital Theatre's first installment was the English Touring Theatre's *Far from the Madding Crowd,* followed by the Young Vic's production of *The Container,* a play highlighting the plight of illegal immigrants coming to the United Kingdom. The Almeida Theatre's first contribution was Jez Butterworth's *Parlour Song,* and the RSC's first entry, *A Comedy of Errors,* was launched in March of 2010.

Robert Delamere, himself a theatre director, has argued that the digital recordings are not meant as rivals to the live theatre event but as a way to "create a mirror of living theatre."[6] The digital production team, which works in consort with the artistic staff of the theatre, uses up to thirteen cameras and edits two performances into a download version.[7] Critics have responded favorably,[8] and, while not capturing the exact sense of a live event, the Digital Theatre recordings—through their adroit shift of camera angles and sequence editing—have offered a version of the theatre event that supersedes the typical recorded versions of staged plays, broadcasts infamous for stiff formality and lack of vitality. The company's recording of *The Container* served as something of a test case for the Digital Theatre. The Young Vic production was a nontraditional one, with audience members and cast stationed together in a cargo container. Despite the unusually intimate confines of this performance space, the digital production succeeded in capturing a sense of the play's claustrophobia and emotional impact. David Lan, artistic director of the Young Vic, affirmed the results: "We thought if Digital Theatre can make this work, they can do anything. And they have."[9]

The ultimate success of such digital ventures in the British theatre remains an open question. No doubt they offer many advantages—the productions allow viewers the opportunity to see first-class productions without the cost of travel to London; the recordings will go into archival holdings that will prove a rich resource for theatre scholars; and the format allows viewers who might never otherwise have the opportunity to engage with theatre. Delamere, in fact, reports that his Digital Theatre venture has reached the global marketplace, used in over 106 countries.[10] He relates receiving glowing e-mails from African schoolteachers, who say they never believed they would be able to share such performances with their students. A sanguine attitude toward these undertakings was expressed by Jonathan Kestenbaum, chief executive of National Endowment for Science, Technology, and the Arts: "Through new digital technologies the performing arts have an exciting opportunity to reach wider audiences and generate new revenue streams. This is a prime example of how new technology can help change the dynamic of a traditional sector, bringing benefits to all."[11] In its early manifestations, one may conclude that the British theatre has enjoyed success and rich potential with its new media engagement, that the dire warnings against "webs and networks" were unwarranted.

While the digital phenomenon sweeping British theatre promises new opportunity and a revitalization of the London entertainment industry, questions emerge as to the long-term effect of such enterprises and the impact of media infiltration on live performance. On the one hand, technical innovations have by and large been embraced by theatre practitioners through the centuries (from the flat-wing groove to body microphones). Nick Hytner, artistic director of the National Theatre, reminds us that a Gilbert and Sullivan opera was once promoted and marketed on the basis "that it was lit by electricity."[12] And in his now classic work on theatre phenomenology, *Great Reckonings in Little Rooms,* Bert States emphasizes the theatre's capacity for appropriation, viewing theatre as a kind of great performative maw that constantly ingests all things new; States recalls the initially unsettling effect that stage furniture had on audiences in the early days of realism.[13] Many scholars have noted this aspect, that theatre has always been quick to employ the technology at hand; however, the digital infiltration has generated an anxiety of a different dimension in theatre artists, who question the digital's impact on theatre's nature, its function as a form, and its place in a globalized society. While Kustow's initial concern about theatre in the twenty-first century may seem knee-jerk and naïve, misplaced in light of successful digitalized theatre enterprises, profound questions remain as to the future and function of theatre, as digital connections crisscross the globe, engendering new social (and economic) relations. In fact, some practitioners regard traditional theatre practice as obsolete. Given the preponderance of media technology and digital interface, Britain's Forced Entertainment company, which employs media heavily in its productions, has argued that story-based, narrative theatre no longer can reach an audience, that its methods are out of sync in a media-saturated culture. The company is forthrightly iconoclastic in its aims, voicing views that defenders of conventional theatre practice would regard as preemptory if not hostile—the company has spoken of theatre as a toy, one to be broken.[14] Such posturing heightens the perception that theatre is experiencing a time of radical change, if not outright assault.

As the year 2009 witnessed the unprecedented alliance of theatre and media, it also saw Britain in an acute time of self-questioning and apprehension. This year viewed the country in the downward spiral of a global recession—the banking crisis brought record foreclosures and layoffs. The British involvement in Afghanistan also triggered renewed skepticism and critique, as casualties spiked over the summer months. Gordon Brown and the Labour Party continued to experience a plummet in poll numbers, indicating citizen disenchantment with the efficacy of government and public leadership. As almost a kind of emblematic event, news outlets reported the death of the last surviving British soldier of World War I, Harry Patch, who died at the age of 111.[15] Geraint Anderson spoke to the dispirited aspect of these times in his article "City of God(less),"[16] which cites the cynical nature of the City (the London financial center) and its mercenary outlook, as the country suffered economic instability and lost savings. Anderson's piece voices the sense of things gone awry, of the individual victimized by forces beyond control (and a nation beyond its prime).

It is telling that Anderson's article emphasizes the value of "moral qualms," in respect to the lack of responsibility manifest by the British financial sector. He continues with this pronouncement: "The spiritual man will not thrive in the City as well as the ruthless, cynical man."[17] Anderson's reference to a moral dimension points to my current research interest in the ethical and spiritual dimension of recent British theatre. And I here wish to place the burgeoning phenomenon of mediatization—and the anxiety that it has produced—in a context of broader disturbance and query, one that involves shifting conceptions of humanity, creativity, and connectedness. Given that Britain in the twenty-first century exists as a global capital, a nexus of media and finance, one of the most variegated and multicultural places on earth, its theatre and culture offer a rich site of investigation in the articulation of value and meaning. The upsurge in theatre's mediatization can be brought into a broader analysis of how we conceive the human's place in the world. Given that the present is a time of skepticism, questioning the viability of free-market capitalism, of fundamentalist imperatives, of ideological political commitments, the theatre's turn to mediatization (for advocates and detractors) points to a new way of constructing national, global, and personal relations. On some level this innovation exhibits the British theatre's attempt not just to gain new audience and market share, but to actualize a new social relation, a new understanding of "being with" the other, which may have multivalent ethical, political, and spiritual dimensions.

It is clear that much is at stake in the discussion of theatre, media, and performance, as the theatre, however construed, participates in the staging and expression of the human. What has resulted, consequently, is not simply a media rivalry but competing conceptions of humanity and ethical imagining. Anxieties over performance and technology connect to wider uneasiness with a rapidly shifting world, what Zygmunt Bauman has characterized as liquid times,[18] a condition whose rapidity of change outpaces understanding and political redress. Given this state of affairs, deep ambivalences emerge as to how to chart and negotiate the future—how to evaluate performance modalities and their potential for an improved world.

In the context of a liquid life, the contestation over the varying merits of the digital and the live in essence participates in a wider debate over political, moral, and spiritual value in the contemporary moment. Those who regard with suspicion the British theatre's turn to digital delivery can point to the darker consequences of global communication networking, which, as Fredric Jameson has argued,[19] serves as a consumer-directed vehicle for the delivery of product and an income source for multinational corporations. In this light, the British theatre produces commodites for the neoliberal global economy, one that looks askance at third-world labor conditions and environmental regulation. For some critics, such globalization has served less to bring goods and services to the world at large than to concentrate power and capital in the hands of the few.[20] Globalization has, moreover, often imperiled local culture, transmitting standards of taste that support the broadest—and most profitable—denominators.

It is significant that many theorists of mediatization, most notably Philip Auslander, conceive of the phenomenon in cultural materialist terms, inflected with neo-Marxist presumptions. In this light, individuals—and, by extension, audience members—are the byproducts of cultural networks and economic consumption. Spectators cannot help but view theatre, according to Auslander, through a televisual lens, as all individuals have become inculturated in televisual society; the viewing pattern is in this sense inescapable. Auslander writes: "In other words, if television once could be seen as ranking among a number of vehicles for conveying expression or information from which we could choose, we no longer have that choice: the televisual has become an intrinsic and determining element of our cultural formation."[21] In her *Theatre in a Media Culture,* which analyzes how media effects have infiltrated American stage performance, Amy Petersen Jensen reiterates this aspect of Auslander's outlook, as her study focuses on "this idea of mediatization acting as an internal mechanism or influence."[22]

What has thus often emerged in articulations of mediatization is the notion of a passive and malleable viewer, a position that highlights the power of systems and the diminishment of individual autonomy. And it is not surprising that certain critical discussion has chafed at this kind of materialist methodology, as this outlook decenters and shortchanges the notion of the human (and aspects of agency and nonmaterial dimension). Ethical philosopher Jean-Luc Nancy typifies the resistance to this functionalist outlook. Nancy has long been fascinated by the nature of human community, and while he asserts that the naming of any one defining quality of human-belonging cannot and should not be attempted, he adamantly opposes the basic Marxist position that humans are what they do—that the human is a product of work and economic relations. For Nancy, the equation of the human element with an economic function (or any activity for that matter) deforms the notion of human uniqueness and the inviolability of its singularity.[23]

In discussions of the live and the mediatized, one often notes the tendency toward adversarial and dichotomized worldviews. Advocates of new media technology champion its vast potential for new communicative modes and experiences; they often regard technology as a path to utopia. Detractors see new media with suspicion, not only as tools that introject consumerist desire but as machinery that reorients human connections. Kershaw insightfully notes that theatre has come to see itself as a defender of perennial values and the human spirit. In this sense the stage assumes for itself the status of a protector, offering a sort of sanctuary that would keep the dubious forces of technological instrumentality at bay. As Kershaw observes, "theatre may seem like the last bastion of the truly human."[24]

In his recent book *Digital Performance,* Steve Dixon acknowledges that digital technology has brought with it justifiable suspicion, of an overbearing authority and agencies of institutional control. Questions of replication, simulacra, and commodity can produce nightmarish visions of the future, in the mode of *Bladerunner.* He also recognizes the anxiousness that can arise when proponents of new technologies speak of a post-human order, of hybrids and androids that may emerge and transform with unlimited horizons.[25] However, for Dixon, the digital world is not one to be feared; rather, it should be embraced and pursued, as a source of creativity and beneficent possibility. Dixon's assessment works against the bleaker charges aimed at the new media and its prospects, arguing that the digital can prove a pathway to truth.

The British theatre's turn to mediatization, as well as the debate it has elicited, in large measure has thus drawn its energy from the broader conversation regarding the future relation between the technological and the human. This essay's aim is not to come down on the side of one or the other; rather, it seeks to emphasize how mediatization functions as a kind of flashpoint, and how the offering of different rhetorics and defenses derives from different philosophical positions and attitudes toward definitions of the human. The matter of employing various media technologies within actual performances, and subsequently using digital networking to deliver performance content, puts a significant question before the British theatre—to what degree does it embrace such technology and its possible post-human implications, or does it remain within a conventional mode of stage practice and risk a reactionary kind of withdrawal or isolation?

To highlight the British theatre's turn to mediatization and to examine the divergent positions it has elicited (and the anxiety it has generated), this essay draws attention to two productions proximate to the launching of the National Theatre Live project, productions that conveyed starkly oppositional attitudes toward technology and the future: J. B. Priestley's *Time and the Conways,* which ran concurrently with *Phèdre* at the National Theatre, and Jez Butterworth's *Jerusalem,* which premiered at the Royal Court that same month. Both the National and the Royal Court have been instrumental in advancing digital interaction for the London theatre; yet, in these productions we note widely divergent uses of and regards for media technologies. What one sees in putting these productions side by side is a rhetorical debate within the London theatre as to the future of performance modalities, and conceptions of the human (and one might add dimensions of spirituality).

Stephen Daldry's wildly successful National Theatre production of Priestley's *An Inspector Calls* in 1992 brought renewed attention to Priestley's work, making this particular period piece seem vibrant and contemporary. In the summer of 2009, the National revived another of

Priestley's plays, *Time and the Conways,* staged by the up-and-coming director Rupert Goold. The piece did have timely implications—the work dramatizes the Conway family's travails between the wars and the period's economic downturn; the text cites "loops" and "slumps" in the markets. The play also questions the state and direction of the nation. Most importantly Priestley's work casts the family drama within a philosophical frame informed by J. W. Dunne's theories of simultaneity and continuum. In short, the suffering and discouragement of the family is set against a somewhat metaphysical backdrop, which functions as a source of solace and significance for the human realm.

Priestley's play follows a three-act structure, with the first set in 1919, a party scene that dramatizes the vitality and aspirations of Mrs. Conway and her near-adult children. The family members play a game of charades and speculate on their futures—Madge seeks a life of political activism and quotes socialistic polemics; Kay dreams of becoming a novelist; Robin makes an unexpected return from the just-concluded war and points to a bright future in sales. Act 2 shifts to 1938 and depicts the family coming together to confront Mrs. Conway about her dwindling resources and need to sell the family home. In turn, we see each character facing disappointment and shortcomings. Madge slaves as a headmistress; Kay is now a hack writer of entertainment columns. Marriages are unhappy, and the future is unremittingly bleak. Kay laments, "There's a great devil in the universe, and we call it Time,"[26] which prompts a philosophical response from her brother Alan, one that conveys Priestley's rather mystical conception of time and futurity. Alan states, "Time's only a kind of a dream, Kay. . . . Time doesn't destroy anything. It merely moves us on—in this life—from one peep-hole to the next" (119). He continues: "we're only a cross-section of our real selves. What we really are is the whole stretch of ourselves, all our time, and when we come to the end of this life, all those selves, all our time, will be us, the real you, the real me." Kay responds with this question: "As if we're—immortal beings?" (119).

Act 3 returns the family to 1918, and we witness occurrences that prefigure their life disappointment. The play concludes reflectively, keenly aware of loss, yet affirmative of an otherworldly frame that secures meaning.

Reviewers noted that Goold's direction of the play was by and large conventional, save for technological flourishes that concluded each act (suggesting the high-tech directorial style of Katie Mitchell).[27] At the end of act 1, the Lyttelton theatre's proscenium, which is convertible, shrank to the size of a small screen—about six feet by four feet framing Kay, who froze in place, giving the moment a cinematic effect. At the end of act 2, the household interior broke open and a string of seven mirror fireplaces, with seven images of Kay, appeared side by side. The conclusion of the play witnessed a stunning display of live and digital interaction, with performers dancing within and next to their projected, motion-tracked images, while recorded lines of text echoed.

The intention and impact of the National Theatre production involved visually conveying an altered, multidimensional reality, in which selves found coherence and import. Significantly, many critics read this high-tech evocation of the otherworldly as inorganic to the play. Michael Billington saw this "mysticism" as an extra ingredient.[28] That said, Goold's choices, I believe, are telling, inasmuch as he deployed media devices for an optimistic, even spiritual vision. As one critic explained, Goold's direction emphasized the "spookiness of the time theories as evidence of cosmic arrangements beyond our understanding."[29] In this line, the future is not to be feared but embraced. The technological aspect of the production thus functioned as the visual metonym of a hopeful future.

If we see an emphatic and optimistic embrace of the digitized in the National production, the Royal Court premiere of Jez Butterworth's *Jerusalem* conveyed a deep suspicion of new media technology and celebrated a return to the woods and a life of pagan spirit. It is curious that both *Time and the Conways* and *Jerusalem* cite the Blake poem of that name, which provided the lyrics for the national hymn of England. Such allusion suggests a verdant England of ideals and promise. Butterworth, however, emphasizes the tawdry, commercialized, and enervated aspect of the present-day nation. The play's depiction of new technology associates such innovation with diminishment, suggesting that advancement into the future only heightens the sense of an ever-receding vitality in the past.

Butterworth's sprawling play depicts the rebel drug dealer Johnny Byron pitted against the bourgeois villagers who seek to drive him from his caravan home in the woods (in order to make way for a housing development). Johnny elicits audience sympathy with his swaggering bravura and tales of reckless adventure. He ignores the threats of the established order and acts as a kind of pied piper to the youths of the area, who find with him safe haven for drinking and drugs. He summons the teenagers to join with him in his defiance and charms them with his spiel: "we will rise up and ride on Salisbury, Marlborough, Devizes, Calne, until the whole plain of Wiltshire dances to the tune of our misrule."[30]

It is telling that we first view Johnny with anachronistic accoutrement. He wears goggles from World War II and carries an old "loudhailer." His trailer is outfitted with "an old hand-cranked air-raid siren" (6). He listens to vinyl albums on a hi-fi set. Butterworth sets his central figure in clear opposition to the media-savvy youths who visit his caravan. Johnny is proudly out of step. In a comic element indicative of his exuberant eccentricity, the audience learns that he has smashed his television set. However, this act is not shown on stage. Rather, Johnny staggers into the morning from his trailer, finding fragments of his television in the grass; only later, when one of the teenagers plays back the recorded sequence on his mobile phone, does Johnny recall that he had in fact destroyed his TV the night before, in a drunken show of irrepressible vitality.

While this use of a cell-phone video produces a comic moment, other instances in the play cast digital technology in a more sinister light. At the play's outset, when the police come to post the eviction order on Johnny's caravan door, they do so while continually operating a camrecorder—the device inflects a sense of surveillance and persecution. Johnny's friend Ginger tells of a recent episode in which Johnny got into trouble for antics caught on a pub's closed-circuit TV. And later in the play we learn that cell phones had been employed by Johnny's teenage followers in an act of violation and betrayal; when they one evening found him passed out intoxicated, having soiled himself, they urinated on him and took photos, later circulating the images among friends via their mobile phones.

Critics have labeled Butterworth's play a pastoral, and certainly there is a strong sense of antipathy toward things modern, toward what Johnny perceives as an insipid media and a numbing corporate consumerism. We learn that the floats for the imminent St. George festival exhibit movie themes, from *The Lord of the Rings* and *Men in Black*. Wesley the pub manager has been enjoined by his corporate bosses to costume as a Morris dancer. When he performs a desultory dance—for cocaine—in front of Johnny and his protégé, Lee, Wesley's humiliation and obeisance are clear. When Wesley asks what they think of his performance, Lee responds, "I need to radically rethink my values" (56).

Reviewer Michael Billington has described *Jerusalem* as a "vision of a vanished demonic magic,"[31] and certainly strong elements of folk ritual and wood sprites pervade the play. Butterworth's evocation of a pagan vitality operates in contrast to his depiction of contemporary banalities and the encroachment of globalizing forces. Johnny repeatedly makes reference to a Druid past, with "ley lines" that once changed the earth. In one of the play's most engaging sequences, he tells a wild tale of once meeting a giant who helped build Stonehenge, and having received from him a drum as a gift—banging on the drum, Johnny relates, would at any time bring the giant to his aid.

The play's romantic affection for the folkways of the past informed the physical design of the production. It is telling that the staging of *Je-*

rusalem strongly employed the rhetoric of the real. An actual caravan trailer occupied the back of the stage, shrouded by real tree limbs. The floor of the stage was covered with dirt. Live chickens roosted beneath the trailer, prompting one reviewer to describe the stage items as "hyper-real exhibits from the countryside."[32] At one point Johnny held up a live turtle that a customer had used for barter in a drug purchase. While the production avoided any kind of high-tech flourish comparable to that seen in *Time and the Conways,* the staging did draw attention to a different sensory effect. When the show began, the house filled with the scent of pine trees and wood smoke. Later, when local yobs beat Johnny and branded him with an iron, the theatre was suffused with a pungent scent meant to signify singed skin.

If one regards Butterworth's play as a statement on the present and the impact of mediatization, then the unquestioned embrace of new communication technologies should give us pause, as should the operation of global networks and market economies. Butterworth indicts facile materialism and celebrates aspects of the human that defy bounds. In this light, the powerful closing image of the play offers quite a compelling statement on mediatization. The bleeding Johnny at the end draws forth the drum and manically pounds its skin—the play thus ends with a kind of invocation, a calling of the gods, via the most basic of communication devices.

It is telling that *Time and the Conways* and *Jerusalem* both conclude with a technological flourish (one digital and one primitive), and in both cases the moment suggests a trajectory to another realm. In a strong sense, both share a profound disquiet with the present. While the production of Priestley's play embraces new technology, as a hopeful, almost ecstatic kind of passage to a selfhood of plenitude, and in effect welcomes the future, *Jerusalem* mistrusts digital culture and expresses yearnings for past mythic connections. Both are in some sense fantastic, driven by escapist impulses. And in these works one sees the confluence of anxieties, pertaining to the market, the media, and the metaphysical. At their core is the question of humanity's dimension and direction and instrumentals of determination.

Mediatization for British theatre and culture represents a crisis not only of representation but of perception, as to how humanity inhabits the world. Baz Kershaw notes that in different historical eras something beyond and not part of the theatrical frame has often been drawn upon to revitalize the theatre form, to "preserve it, restore it, or connect it to some other domain."[33] And Kershaw views digital technologies in this light, as a positive, as in some sense giving theatre new life, offering the possibility of a multifaceted Bauhaus sensorium.[34] Others have taken oppositional views. In 2005 the Random Dance Company, which had previously relied heavily on media techniques, renounced such effects; Laurie Anderson's 2005 performance at the Barbican witnessed the dismissal of her signature screen images, as Anderson stood alone on the stage with eighty lit candles.[35] Though a strong advocate of digital performance, Dixon acknowledges this kind of resistance and recognizes the ethical dimension of such concerns; he points to the 2003 protest of noted theatre semiotician Patrice Pavis, who passionately pled for a return to the living body, voicing his fear that "technology has got the upper hand of the human for good."[36]

Such diverse perceptions suggest that the issue of mediatization has arrived at no settled conclusion, and, while the British theatre has recently made impressive strides in positioning its work in the digital marketplace, one shall see how this turn impacts its repute and the nature of its work. In the end, debates over the role and use of new media technologies reveal mediatization as something of a cipher, implicated in a contest of competing values and possible human futures.

Notes

1. Baz Kershaw, "Dramas of the Performative Society: Theatre at the End of Its Tether," *New Theatre Quarterly* 17, no.3 (2001): 204, http://books.google.com/books?id=6HrZoVLuk8UC&pg=PA211&lpg=PA211&dq=%22digital+theatre%22+london&source=bl&ots=zjH8v9w-pE&sig=ezIvXlI-WNOkmyZoTaDo9TQ4fb4&hl=en&ei=D7–8S4LQMIvA8wTs6a33Bw&sa=X&oi=book_result&ct=result&resnum=4&ved=0CAsQ6AEwAzge#v=onepage&q=%22digital%20theatre%22%201ondon&f=false.

2. Qtd. in Kershaw, "Dramas of the Performative Society," 210.

3. James C. Taylor, "National Theatre Goes Global with *Phèdre* Broadcast," *Los Angeles Times,* June 28, 2009, http://articles.latimes.com/2009/jun/28/entertainment/ca-nicholas-hytner28.

4. What's Onstage, "Globe Links with ROH for Big Screen Broadcasts," September 23, 2009, http://www.whatsonstage.com/news/theatre/london/E8831253708865/Globe+Links+with+ROH+for+Big+Screen+Broadcasts.html.

5. Stephen Adams, "iTunes for Theatre," *Telegraph,* October 26, 2009, http://www.telegraph.co.uk/culture/theatre/theatre-news/6438716/iTunes-for-theatre-will-offer-plays-for-8.99.html.

6. Qtd. in Adams, "iTunes for Theatre."

7. Bryan Appleyard, "Why Would You Download Plays?" *London Times,* October 25, 2009, http://entertainment.timesonline.co.uk/tol/arts_and_entertainment/stage/theatre/article6884072.ece.

8. Charles Spencer, "Theatre via Your PC—Will It Work?" *Telegraph,* October 27, 2009, http://www.telegraph.co.uk/culture/theatre/theatre-news/6438840/Theatre-via-your-PC-will-it-work.html.

9. Qtd. in Official London Theatre, "Leading Theatres Launch Downloadable Shows," October 26, 2009, http://www.officiallondontheatre.co.uk/news/latest/view/item107946/&t=Leading%20theatres%20launch%20downloadable%20shows.

10. Josh Spero, "Digital Theatre: From Page to Stage to Screen," *The Arts Desk,* February 24, 2010, http://www.theartsdesk.com/index.php?option=com_k2&view=item&id=1068:digital-theatre&Itemid=25.

11. "New Research Reveals Audience Thirst for 'Digital Theatre,'" February 2, 2010, NESTA, http://www.nesta.org.uk/press_releases/assets/features/new_research_reveals_audience_thirst_for_digital_theatre.

12. Qtd. in Anne Nicholson Weber, *Upstaged: Making Theatre in the Media Age* (New York: Routledge, 2006), 1.

13. Bert States, *Great Reckonings in Little Rooms: On the Phenomenology of Theater* (Berkeley: University of California Press, 1985), 41–42.

14. See Jonathan Kalb, "Amazing Untold Stories of Catalogues," *PAJ: A Journal of Performance and Art* 31, no. 2 (May 2009): 3, http://muse.jhu.edu/journals/performing_arts_journal/v031/31.2.kalb.html.

15. Tracy McVeigh and Mark Townsend, "Harry Patch, Britain's Last Surviving Soldier of the Great War, Dies at 111," *Guardian,* July 26, 2009, http://www.guardian.co.uk/world/2009/jul/26/world-war-one-veteran-harry-patch-dies-aged-111.

16. Geraint Anderson, "City of God(less)," *London Paper,* July 24, 2009, 10.

17. Anderson, "City of God(less)," 10.

18. Zygmunt Bauman, *Liquid Times: Living in an Age of Uncertainty* (Cambridge: Polity Press, 2007), 1.

19. Fredric Jameson, "Notes on Globalization as a Philosophical Issue," in *The Cultures of Globalization,* ed. Fredric Jameson and Masao Miyoshi (Durham: Duke University Press, 1998), 54–56.

20. Richard De Zoysa and Otto Newman, "Globalization, Soft Power and the Challenge of Hollywood," *Contemporary Politics* 8, no. 3 (2002): 186–87, http://web.ebscohost.com/ehost/pdfviewer/pdfviewer?hid=106&sid=0a22c3b4-3657-4060-8b19-20efe076aa8c%40sessionmgr111&vid=5.

21. Philip Auslander, *Liveness: Performance in a Mediatized Culture* (New York: Routledge, 1999), 2.

22. Amy Petersen Jensen, *Theatre in a Media Culture: Production, Performance and Perception since 1970* (London: McFarland, 2007), 2.

23. Fred *Dallmayr,* "An 'Inoperable' Global Community? Reflections on Nancy," in *On Jean-Luc Nancy,* ed. Darren Sheppard, Simon Sparks, and Colin Thomas (New York: Routledge, 1997), 174–96.

24. Kershaw, "Dramas of the Performative Society," 210.

25. Steve Dixon, *Digital Performance: A History of New Media in Theater, Dance, Performance Art, and Installation* (Cambridge, MA: MIT Press, 2007), 147–54.

26. J. B. Priestley, *Time and the Conways,* in *Six Plays* (London: Heinemann, 1979), 118. Subsequent text references are to pages of this edition.

27. John Thaxter, "Time and the Conways," *The Stage,* May 6, 2009, http://www.thestage.co.uk/reviews/review.php/24319/time-and-the-conways.

28. Michael Billington, "Time and the Conways," *Guardian,* May 6, 2009, http://www.guardian.co.uk/stage/2009/may/06/time-conways-review-priestley.

29. Michael Coveney, "Time and the Conways," *Independent,* May 11, 2009, http://www.independent.co.uk/arts-entertainment/theatre-dance/reviews/time-and-the-conways-national-theatre-london-1682500.html.

30. Jez Butterworth, *Jerusalem* (London: Nick Hern Books, 2009), 52. Subsequent text references are to pages of this edition.

31. Michael Billington, "Jerusalem, Royal Court," *Guardian,* July 16, 2009, http://www.guardian.co.uk/stage/2009/jul/16/jerusalem-review.

32. Susannah Clapp, "Jerusalem," *Observer,* July 19, 2009, http://www.guardian.co.uk/stage/2009/jul/19/jerusalem-royal-court-review.

33. Kershaw, "Dramas of the Performative Society," 204.

34. Ibid., 211.

35. Dixon, *Digital Performance,* 645–47.

36. Qtd. in Dixon, *Digital Performance,* 650.

Nollywood

Film and Home Video, or the Death of Nigerian Theatre

Becky Becker

NIGERIAN AUTHORS Chinua Achebe, Wole Soyinka, and Femi Osofisan, among others, have brought welcome acclaim to a country plagued by a corrupt young government, unwieldy infrastructural problems, violence linked to oil, and, most recently, violence linked to religion. While such challenges have inspired individual writers, perhaps it is more surprising that the volatile situation in Nigeria has allowed a film and home video industry to develop and flourish. Yet, over the past two decades, "film" has become a burgeoning business there—particularly in its behemoth former capital, Lagos. Having visited various parts of the country on a faculty development seminar in May 2008,[1] I left with the impression that the film and home video industry has had a disastrous impact on live theatre, despite its dependence on Nigerian theatrical tradition for its very existence. A return to its theatrical origins may be exactly what Nollywood needs to bring Nigeria the kind of recognition this young nation craves.[2]

The term "Nollywood" was first used in 2002 by Matt Steinglass in a *New York Times* article discussing a self-imposed "recess" Nigerian video makers enacted that year due to overproduction. According to Steinglass, quality and sales in the largely Igbo-controlled video market had diminished to such an extent that industry heads agreed to the recess in order to examine problems and discuss solutions. In the same article, Steinglass points out the tendency of Yoruba filmmakers to separate themselves from Igbo video makers, which may help to explain conflicting histories claimed by different segments of the film and video industry.[3] The Yoruba legacy appears to be more directly linked to traditional Nigerian theatre practitioners, like Hubert Ogunde, as well as a more artistic approach to film; in contrast, the Igbo legacy of moving directly to video seems to take a more market- and audience-driven approach. While Lagos is a cosmopolitan city populated by people from all over Nigeria, in addition to many other Africa nations and countries across the world, two of Nigeria's largest ethnic groups lay claim to Nollywood's uncertain legacy.

One important lineage acknowledges Nollywood's connection to the traditional Yoruba Traveling Theatre movement championed by theatre director Chief Hubert Ogunde. Typically, Nigeria's film industry is traced back to the 1979 film *Aiye*, directed by Ola Balogun and based on Ogunde's original play pitting a traditional medicine man against an evil witch doctor.[4] A decade later, however, another lineage was fostered through the Igbo-language film *Living in Bondage* (1988), directed by Chris Obi Rapu, and credited with bringing home video to the wider attention of the Nigerian people. Depicting a man who is promised success by a secret cult if he is willing to sacrifice his wife, *Living in Bondage* was filmed in Igbo with English subtitles and released directly to video. It was among the first financially successful home videos in Nigeria and seems to have been the spark that ignited the rapid-fire subsequent growth of Nollywood.[5]

Film critic Femi Shake acknowledges Nollywood's connection to the "second generation of scholars [in Nigeria] who were trained in the theatre arts," but also points to an earlier source—the mobile cinema, which got its start in Lagos in 1925. According to Shake, Lagos Chief Health Officer William Sellers used film during a major epidemic outbreak to educate the people of Lagos, under colonial rule, who thought the plague was brought there by non-Lagosians. Film allowed Sellers to show the people of Lagos that the illness was caused by unhygienic conditions, rather than foreigners.[6] Nosa Owens-Ibie concurs with the film industry's origin as a propaganda tool for Sellers's Colonial Film Unit; however, he points to film's beginnings even earlier in Nigeria's history, noting that "[t]he first film screenings in Nigeria took place at Glover Memorial Hall, Lagos" in August 1903. Although Nigerian Herbert Macaulay managed the screening, it was presented for dignitaries visiting from Spain,[7] setting a precedent for foreign involvement in Nigerian film.[8] Even the first successful feature film recorded in a Nigerian language (Igbo), *Amadi*, in 1975, was produced by filmmaker Balogun, who had returned to Nigeria in 1973, following his film training in France, to found the film production company Afrocult Foundation Limited.[9] Balogun is also credited with helping popular Nigerian theatre companies transition from live theatre to film.[10] Ripe with complexity, the dueling

Nollywood histories presented here indicate Nigeria's desire to discover its own legacy unfettered by outside influences.

While divergent histories of video and film in Nigeria are important to examine, a common perception of Nollywood, both in Nigeria and abroad, seems to be that it is somehow indicative of or linked to overarching stereotypes of Nigerians that permeate the globe more generally. One has only to look to the recent Oscar-nominated film *District Nine* to understand that Nigerians are fair game for ridicule.[11] Nigeria is perceived to be the land of Internet scams, oil militants, and get-rich-quick ploys. More recently, brutal violence between Christians and Muslims in northern Nigeria, and perhaps most notably from the Detroit "Christmas Day terrorist," has further alienated Nigerians from the "civilized" world.[12] While I do not intend to underestimate the impact each ethnic group's film history may have on the perception of Nollywood as a primarily entertainment-focused industry versus an artistry-focused industry, I do think that Nigeria's global reputation is an important perspective to keep in mind, at least for the moment.

It is within this global context, after all, that Nollywood received its name. Although naming can sometimes be an exercise in glibness, it is also one of the ways in which people, events, and institutions are defined. In that regard, it seems clear that Nollywood has, however slickly, been placed within the context of Hollywood first and foremost, which, I would argue, assumes a primary focus on entertainment rather than artistry, as does its link to Bollywood, another developing world film and video industry.[13] Yet with the third-largest film industry after Hollywood and Bollywood (and, incidentally, the second-largest industry in Nigeria after oil), perhaps the most troubling aspect of its name is the automatic comparison made to trades that are larger and possess much longer histories. There are distinct differences among the top three film industries and their cultures that may outweigh any similarities. It is these differences—and, more particularly, the perspective of Nigerian critics on the country's film industry, as well as its impact on Nigerian theatre—that draw my interest.

As a model for popular entertainment worldwide, Hollywood produces around 630 films each year—many of them intended blockbusters aimed at achieving record audiences and popular acclaim. Bollywood produces approximately eight hundred films per year on much smaller budgets, making films that tend to be forty minutes longer than the average one-hundred-minute Hollywood blockbuster in the same amount of time—around forty days.[14] In contrast, Nollywood mass-produces up to two thousand videos each year. Nigeria's most prolific director, Chico

Ejiro, boasts eighty films directed over an eight-year period and claims to be able to finish production on a film in as little as three days.[15] Given this rapacious production rate, there is something unique going on in Nigerian film and entertainment that makes it incomparable to other film and video industries.

One compelling difference in Nigeria's film history is its lineage, which does appear to have a direct link to Nigerian theatre. The Yoruba-language Traveling Theatre movement brought popular and often subversively political entertainment to people throughout the country for several decades, and according to Moradewun Adejunmobi, some companies even turned to television as a means of survival as early as the 1960s.[16] Calling it "the most populist dramaturgy Nigeria ever experienced," Awam Amkpa describes this Traveling Theatre as an important arbiter between British colonial rule and independence.[17] Traveling Theatre not only provided a carnival aesthetic of music and dance intertwined with a moralistic plot, but "Yoruba Traveling Theatre also opened up a process of desiring, in which acts of remembering and memorializing native traditions, reinventing cultural reality, and weaving discourses of anticolonial nationalism gave people a collective sense of selfhood independent of England's colonial rule."[18] With independence in 1960, a greater sense of cosmopolitanism emerged, and accordingly, "companies began to adapt European and American performance conventions once rejected by anticolonial nationalists of pre-independence."[19] As the need for the companies' political underpinnings diminished, so too did the Yoruba Traveling Theatre's impact. Paired with developing dangers as oil militants made travel throughout the country treacherous, changes in Nigeria's political and cultural landscape eventually brought an end to Traveling Theatre.[20]

Recognizing the Yoruba Traveling Theatre's shrinking appeal, Ogunde, one of its celebrated fathers, seems to have turned to celluloid in order to regain his theatre's populist appeal. While celluloid did not prove to be the answer, perhaps video—with its economic production and accessibility—is the contemporary Nigerian answer to the theatre's diminished impact. Noting that "outside the country . . . Nollywood is a mere curio," film critic Onookome Okome reflects: "In Nigeria, Nollywood is popular because it speaks to aspects of social life that many people live. It speaks to and debates social and cultural anxieties the way no other media had done before. It gestures to political discourse in a very surreptitious manner. It invests the individual, especially the individual living in the city, with a new sense of person."[21] Okome's description of Nollywood's rough-and-tumble video industry sounds much like Amkpa's characterization of the Yoruba Traveling Theatre and its necessity as a link to national identity for audiences in colonial Nigeria.

Some film critics make an even more direct link between Nigerian theatre and the film and video industry, pointing to aesthetic qualities embraced by Nollywood producers and filmmakers. As Ahmed Yerima suggests, "The relationship between the Nigerian film and the dramatic institution is that the art of performance of dramatization comes from theatre and we capture aspects of it with a camera, take it to the studio for production. And if you look at it critically, you find out that the Nigerian film is almost the same as the Nigerian theatre."[22] While Yerima's description may sound overly simplistic, having watched portions of Nollywood videos and television, both while visiting Nigeria and here at home, I find that there is validity in this statement. The videos often include just one camera angle (or very few), minimal cuts from shot to shot, and, in many cases, filmed-through scenes, much like a play that has been filmed for television or purposely created to preserve its theatrical qualities.

Nigerian critics seem to be split in their responses to Nollywood. While some, like Okome, defend its youth in the film- and video-making industry, others see this as a poor excuse for maintaining the status quo. Kole Omotoso goes so far as to say, "People are going to begin to feel ashamed of doing these things, they will look at the thing and say, how could I have done this."[23] Omotoso's outlook suggests that there will come a point when Nigerian film and video artists recognize the need for increased integrity in aesthetic value. Taking a more pragmatic view, Emeka Nwabueze recognizes "a situation where the movies have become highly predictable. It was a period of maturation and inevitably fraught with repetition, poor costuming and poor understanding of performance aesthetics. But within that period of performative poverty, there were flickers of light."[24] Flickers of light certainly do exist within Nollywood's short history. But what about home video's impact on live Nigerian theatre? How can Nigeria sustain a live theatre if home video is perceived—at least in some sense—to have taken its place? And why does Nigeria find itself in this situation after sustaining a strong indigenous theatre prior to home video's insurgence?

In his keynote address at the Twentieth Convention of the Society of Nigeria Theatre Artists (SONTA) in July 2006, playwright Femi Osofisan discussed the state of Nigerian theatre. Titling his talk "Theatrical Life after the Generals: or Nigerian Theatre in Search of a Lifeline," Osofisan's outlook on theatre is quite bleak. Perhaps it is telling that his address was published in a book called *Trends in the Theory and Practice of Theatre in Nigeria*, printed in Nigeria in 2008. In a book ostensibly focused on theatre, the two lead articles discuss current trends in film. In his address Osofisan points to a number of reasons for the theatre's demise, such as the country's quick plunge in the late 1970s from oil boom to "oil doom," and the insecurity of the country's economy and infrastructure that followed. In rapid succession, a number of theatrical greats were lost, such as Ogunde, Duro Ladipo, and Ola Rotimi, among others. Their deaths seem to mark the loss of a galvanizing force needed to continue the theatrical tradition. Perhaps even more disturbing is the loss of theatrical activity in Nigeria to crime: with the rise of poverty and crime rates, Nigerians took to their houses, and continue even now to avoid going out after nightfall. The result of this situation, according to Osofisan, has serious consequences on all Nigerian art: "Our art from all appearances, is in the throes of extinction."[25] He continues: "The production of plays[—]I am talking of 'production' here in its two connotations, as the creation of scripts as well as the realization of these scripts on stage—has dwindled dangerously among our people. The few theatres that exist have grown dilapidated out of neglect or are being converted to other uses, most often wedding ceremonies."[26] Indeed, while visiting Nigeria in 2008, I encountered exactly the conditions Osofisan describes—and not in a small regional or community theatre, but in the Nigerian National Theatre—Lagos's pride and joy during its 1977 hosting of the Second World Black and African Festival of Arts and Culture (FESTAC 77). While we were treated to a viewing of the FESTAC archives, tentatively held under poor conditions in the basement of the theatre, a wedding ceremony and party were being held on an upper floor. If memory serves, a rehearsal was in progress in the smaller theatre space housed in the complex, but that space had been turned into a film venue. Reading Osofisan's address after my first visit to Nigeria merely confirmed a situation that was, to me, already apparent.

Given Nigeria's sociopolitical situation—widespread poverty, prohibitive night travel, road hazards, and crime—it makes sense that digital technology would step in to take the place of traditional theatre—at least for a time. However, from Osofisan's perspective, the situation is not merely a temporary fix, but an ongoing condition that serves to undermine the life and potential of Nigerian theatre. Fearing the next generation of would-be theatre practitioners have lost any sense of process, he contends: "Spoilt in the indulgence of Nollywood's predilection for improvisational processes, very few of the actors are still capable of the mental agility required for the learning of lines, and fewer still can sustain the discipline that live theatre demands especially when measured against the poor remuneration that it offers."[27] Not only has Nigeria's precarious sociopolitical situation decimated live theatre, but it has set a

A new Nollywood studio located just outside Calabar, Nigeria: a sign of Nollywood's expansion beyond Lagos, its birthplace. Photo by Becky Becker.

dangerous precedent for future attempts to recover the theatre's power, both as an aesthetic experience for audiences and as a challenging and satisfying craft for actors. One reality that seems to pervade all discussion of the video industry in Nigeria is the sense that it "serves the Nigerian situation."[28] The home video industry is a practical solution for an impoverished, entertainment-hungry public seeking escape in the safety of their own homes. For women in Nigeria, there is an added bonus. Prior to the surge of home video production, women who frequented the cinema were deemed "whores and 'goodtime women.'"[29] With the advent of home video, perhaps in a larger sense, the democratization of art is its greatest achievement—the same quality, some would argue, that is its greatest downfall. According to Okome, however, Nollywood has an inherent value: "I see Nollywood forming as a viable discursive arena in our social history, which is why it is painful to me that no one has tried to collect and archive Nollywood films the way scholars have archived Bollywood and Hollywood. We seem to be repeating the silly history of neglecting the production and consumption of popular culture in Nigeria and indeed Africa."[30] Perhaps ironically, even as Osofisan sees little reason to defend the merits of the home video industry, Okome laments its dismissal as undeserving of scholarly attention. Perhaps most intriguingly, Okome suggests that Nollywood "offers explanation to things we do in the dark. It is eloquent about the life we live but would not speak about in public."[31]

One thing about Nollywood is certain. It is not going away. Not only has it created thousands of jobs significant to the growth of the Nigerian economy, but it also serves a dynamic social purpose in a time of continued unrest. Moreover, Nigerian university theatre programs and their starstruck students alike seem to have accepted film as the inevitable intended pursuit after graduation. One playwright's solution has been to continue his own work as a writer for the theatre, and to join the ranks of Nollywood filmmakers himself. Playwright Samuel Chinedum Ukala chose to transform his play *Akpakaland* into a film so that more people would have access to its message. His agenda also seems to be to reform the existing home video structure, as he asserts here: "Films from the Nigerian home video are mainly naturalistic in their presentation and most of them deal with what one could call trite subject-matters, over-flogged issues that everybody knows about. Some glamorize wicked rituals to the extent of giving the impression that everybody in Nigeria is a witch or wizard, can disappear in a jiffy, or kill human beings to make money. Those things might be in our country, but are they as prevalent as we make them?"[32] Ukala's play is socially relevant with themes of corruption and misrule, demonstrating his desire to provide another storyline for Nigerians to consider, rather than the stereotypical plots of witchcraft or area boy thugs.[33] In discussing his decision to turn the play into a film, Ukala comments: "in our traditional aesthetics, a story is a collaborative thing, a recreation of events by the performer as well as the audience. So it is a question of collaboration, not that of one being a super star and the other being a passive spectator. I tried to use that principle in the filming of *Akpakaland*."[34] While it may be a stretch to imagine filmmaking that creates a collaborative connection with its audience—particularly in light of Nollywood's immature tradition—Ukala's instinct to join the throng is not unique. Many playwrights in Nigeria—and in this country, for that matter—enjoy the widespread appeal that can come from transforming their work for film and video.[35] If accessibility is an issue in Nigeria due to cost and crime, the same may be said for a public who shuns Broadway's outrageous ticket prices. A major difference, however, is that although the majority of Americans may never see a play on Broadway, a strong and diverse infrastructure of theatres they can afford to attend does exist. And Americans are typically unafraid to go out at night to do just that.

Is there a solution to Nigeria's Nollywood? Does it need solving?

Does theatre have a place in Nigeria's cultural landscape? As a believer in the power of "liveness," I would have to say, absolutely. According to Ndubuisi Nnanna, "One of the reasons for the gradual unpopularity of the theatre in Nigeria might be connected with the failure of some of the country's playwrights to locate the pulse of the nation by dealing with such issues of urgent national interest as those arising from the civil war experience as a way of sounding necessary warnings to encourage nationalist feelings, mutual responsibility and national unity."[36] Harkening back to the success of the Yoruba Traveling Theatre, Nnanna's suggestion seems particularly valuable. Perhaps when more film- and video makers begin to abandon stereotypical themes and stories and connect more keenly with the realities of the Nigerian people, theatre will again find its voice. Perhaps it will be through the continued efforts of playwrights like Ukala, writing socially relevant plays and turning them into films for mass consumption, that a new Nigerian theatre tradition will eventually, however slowly, reemerge.

Notes

1. I am grateful to have received funding through both a University System of Georgia Chancellor's Award and Faculty Development grants from Columbus State University in order to participate in the seminar, which focused on the arts of Nigeria.

2. The territories that make up Nigeria were first joined together and named by Lord Lugard under colonial rule. Nigeria gained its independence in 1960 and has continued to experience political unrest during its brief history as an independent nation. Eghosa E. Osaghae, *Crippled Giant: Nigeria Since Independence* (Bloomington: Indiana University Press, 1998), 1, 31.

3. Matt Steinglass, "When There's Too Much of a Not-Very-Good Thing," *New York Times*, May 26, 2002, http://www.nytimes.com/2002/05/26/arts/film-when-there-s-too-much-of-a-not-very-good-thing.html.

4. Manthia Diawara, *African Cinema: Politics and Culture* (Bloomington: Indiana University Press, 1992), 123.

5. William Easterly, *The White Man's Burden* (New York: Penguin, 2006), 102.

6. Femi Okiremuete Shake, "It's Time to Study Film at the Highest Level in Nigeria," *Film Nigeria: An International Journal of the Nigerian Film* 1, no. 1 (First Quarter 2008): 8.

7. A link between these earliest film screenings and the later Yoruba Traveling Theatre may be their initial focus on an elite audience. As Awam Amkpa asserts, "the enthusiastic reception of Ogunde's works by the indigenous elite paved the way for the Yoruba Traveling Theatres." Awam Amkpa, *Theatre and Postcolonial Desires* (New York: Routledge, 2004), 84.

8. Awam Amkpa chronicles the development of the Yoruba Traveling The-

atre, which brought theatre to the people and "stemmed from two traditions of dissent in Nigeria." Tracing it as far back as 1593 to rebel members of the Oyo royal court who espoused the Egungun ritual, as well as connecting it to Nigeria's Nationalist struggle and Nigerian Christians who campaigned for an Africanized Church, Amkpa points to the Yoruba Traveling Theatre as a method of propaganda for social change—similar to the earliest films in Nigeria's colonial history, albeit from a very different perspective. Amkpa, *Theatre and Postcolonial Desires,* 79.

9. Diawara, *African Cinema,* 146–47.

10. Foluke Ogunleye, ed., *African Video Film Today* (Matsapha, Swaziland: Academic Publishers, 2003), 44.

11. Although *District Nine* is set in South Africa, the alien "prawns," as they are called in the film, participate in black-market weapon sales with a group of Nigerians led by a warlord named Mumbo. Basically, the Nigerians in this film are perceived to be violent sellouts. This depiction mimics stereotypical present-day images of Nigerians as oil- and weapon-hungry militants.

12. Mark Whittington, "Terrorist Attack over Detroit Averted on Christmas Day," Associated Content: The People's Media Company, December 26, 2009, http://www.associatedcontent.com/article/2526979/terrorist_attack_over_detroit_averted.html.

13. This is not to say that artistic films come out of none of these industries; in fact, many artfully made films originate in Hollywood and Bollywood, but far more films with a populist and high-dollar-yielding focus are produced in both venues.

14. Karen Russo, "Hollywood, Bollywood to Merge into One Movie Empire?" ABC News/Entertainment Online, June 25, 2008, http://abcnews.go.com/Entertainment/Movies/story?id=5243650&page=1.

15. "The Nollywood Phenomenon," African Movie Channel, 2008, http://www.africanmoviechannel.com/nollywood.asp.

16. Moradewun Adejunmobi, "English and the Audience of an African Popular Culture: The Case of Nigerian Video Film," *Cultural Critique* 50 (Winter 2002): 77.

17. Amkpa, *Theatre and Postcolonial Desires,* 77.

18. Ibid., 76–77.

19. Ibid., 82.

20. More a far-reaching theatrical tradition than a singular company, the Yoruba Traveling Theatre may be equated to the Teatro movement of the 1960s in the United States, which was inspired by a need for legislation to protect migrant workers. While the Teatro movement began with El Teatro Campesino and its founders, Luis Valdez, Dolores Huerta, and Cesar Chavez, it spread quickly to include more than one hundred teatros across the country. Similarly, Hubert Ogunde is often credited with originating the Yoruba Traveling Theatre movement, which developed into a far-reaching tradition in southern Nigeria for several decades. In the United States, the Teatro movement was relatively short-lived by comparison, diminishing after changes in legislation appeared to adequately protect the rights of migrant workers.

21. Onookome Okome, "It Is Difficult to Ignore Nollywood," *Film Nigeria: An International Journal of the Nigerian Film* 1, no. 1 (First Quarter 2008): 6.

22. Ahmed Yerima, "Nigeria Has Only Made a Name in Television Drama," *Film Nigeria: An International Journal of the Nigerian Film* 1, no. 1 (First Quarter 2008): 19.

23. Kole Omotoso, "The Video Film Serves the Nigerian Situation," *Film Nigeria: An International Journal of the Nigerian Film* 1, no. 1 (First Quarter 2008): 23.

24. Emeka Nwabueze, "There Must Be an Intellectual Touch to the Nigerian Film," *Film Nigeria: An International Journal of the Nigerian Film* 1, no. 1 (First Quarter 2008): 33

25. Femi Osofisan, "Keynote Address: Theatrical Life after the Generals: or Nigerian Theatre in Search of a Lifeline," *Trends in the Theory and Practice of Theatre in Nigeria,* ed. Duro Oni and Ahmed Yerima (Lagos: Society of Nigerian Theatre Artists, 2008), xiii.

26. Ibid.

27. Ibid., xxi.

28. Omotoso, "Video Film Serves the Nigerian Situation," 23.

29. Hope Eghagha, "What Has Defined the Tenor of Nollywood Is Commercialism," *Film Nigeria: An International Journal of the Nigerian Film* 1, no. 1 (First Quarter 2008): 7.

30. Okome, "It Is Difficult to Ignore Nollywood," 7.

31. Ibid.

32. Samuel Chinedum Ukala, "Intellectuals Should Show the Way Forward in Film Production," *Film Nigeria: An International Journal of the Nigerian Film* 1, no. 1 (First Quarter 2008): 12.

33. "Area boys" is defined by Lizzie Williams in *Nigeria: The Bradt Travel Guide* (Buckinghamshire, England: Bradt Travel Guides, 2005) as "Lagos hoodlums who steal from people using intimidation" (332). While visiting Lagos, my group had an encounter with several area boys outside a market when they tried to make us pay to park our vehicle. As their name suggests, area boys tend to work a particular quarter of the city, exploiting citizens and foreigners alike.

34. Ukala, "Intellectuals Should Show the Way Forward," 11–12.

35. Nigerian American playwright Tess Onwueme is another whose interests have turned to film. In an unpublished interview I conducted with Onwueme on July 2–3, 2008, she had this to say about moving from writing plays to writing novels: "it looks like I'm at the point where the message cannot wait. And I want to be able—I'm hungry for that communication, that forum to be able to break through those walls to reach as many in that vast audience. That is the global audience. Because I see the space, the global space, as my space. And the theatre—the theatre space for us to dramatize and exchange and share the dialogue and all the issues that pertain to us, as global citizens. As people who have so much in common. But sometimes we don't even realize how so connected we are. And we're separated by so much. The novel gives me an edge, in that sense, and simplifies a little bit. Ideally, where I would like to go is on screen—to go into documentary production. That's my ultimate goal, because then, we'll

be speaking—that opens up. The screen is so much closer to the folklore, you know, oral tradition." Becky Becker, interview with Tess Onwueme, July 2–3, 2008.

Not only does Onwueme perceive a need for the portability of the novel, but film also seems to make the personal connection that theatre can no longer make under the current circumstances. While I remain skeptical, until the volatile situation in Nigeria changes, film may be the closest mode to the oral tradition Nigerians are able to find—particularly in light of new unrest that is likely to bubble up with the recent death of President Umaru Yar'Adua, who had promised peace in the Niger Delta and a better future for Nigeria's millions of impoverished.

36. Ndubuisi Nnanna, "The Nigerian Civil War in Modern Nigerian Drama: Selective Amnesia or Wisdom of the Ostrich," *Trends in the Theory and Practice of Theatre in Nigeria*, ed. Duro Oni and Ahmed Yerima (Lagos: Society of Nigerian Theatre Artists, 2008), 150.

The Performative Nature of Filmed Reproductions of Live Performance

Nathan Stith

> They want us to produce art that solves the problems of the world, and I don't think that art does that very well. I think what we can do is offer people a space in which to reflect upon the problems of the world.
>
> —Coco Fusco to Rosemary Weatherston, "Performing Bodies, Performing Culture: An Interview with Coco Fusco and Nao Bustamente," in *Body Politics and the Fictional Double*, ed. Debra Walker King

> In the twenty-first century, the important questions of identity, morality, and authority have all been transformed by multiculturalism, postmodern politics, and cultural change. While [Sacha] Baron Cohen does not provide any definitive answers, he certainly has found a way to make us sit up and take notice.
>
> —Robert A. Saunders, *The Many Faces of Sacha Baron Cohen: Politics, Parody, and the Battle over Borat*

IN 1992, PERFORMANCE artists Coco Fusco and Guillermo Gómez-Peña created the site-specific performance piece *Two Amerindians Visit . . .*, as part of the Edge '92 Biennial at Columbus Plaza in Madrid, Spain.[1] During the performance, and subsequent reiterations at Covent Garden in London, the Smithsonian in Washington, D.C., the Field Museum in Chicago, and others, Fusco and Gómez-Peña presented themselves as Amerindians who were found in a newly discovered island in the Gulf of Mexico called Guatinau. The performances, along with one-on-one interviews, were recorded by filmmaker Paula Heredia. This video became the documentary *The Couple in the Cage* (1993).[2] In 2006, comedian Sacha Baron Cohen, posing as a faux Kazakhstani journalist, Borat Sagdiyev, traveled across the United States recording his interactions with unsuspecting locals along the way. The filmed exchanges became the 2006 mockumentary *Borat: Cultural Learnings of America for Make Benefit Glorious Nation of Kazakhstan.*[3] In both examples, the live audience is led to believe that the characters created by these artists are not characters but real people. The audiences of the live performances interact with these characters under the false pretense that they are relating to real people. However, in the mediatized reproductions, the audience is aware that the artists have created false personas; they view the documented reproductions with knowledge that the live audience does not have and thus are able to experience the filmed reproductions in ways not available to the live audience. In so doing, these artists are illustrating what Philip Auslander calls "the performativity of performance documentation."[4]

In order to define the concept of performativity, Auslander follows the theory set forth by J. L. Austin in "How to Do Things with Words." Austin asserts that phrases that embody actions, such as stating "I do" during a wedding ceremony, are performatives as opposed to phrases that merely describe something, which he calls constatives.[5] In other words, by speaking the words "I do" one is actually *performing* an action rather than describing an action. In translating this definition from the world of linguistics to that of performance documentation, Auslander notes, "the traditional view sees performance documents as constatives that describe performances and state that they occurred"; however, he proposes that the act of documenting performance art "does not simply generate image/statements that describe an autonomous performance and state that it occurred: it produces an event as a performance."[6]

Auslander uses Richard Bauman's definition of performance in order to clarify this idea. Bauman states, "performance rests on an assumption of responsibility to an audience for a display of communicative virtuosity. . . . In this sense of performance, then, the act of expression itself is framed as display: objectified, lifted out to a degree from its contextual surroundings, and opened up to interpretive and evaluative scrutiny by an audience both in terms of its intrinsic qualities and its associational resonances." However, as Auslander notes, there are holes in the connection between Bauman's definition of performance and his own ideas about the performativity of performance documentation. The most notable discrepancy is with Bauman's opinion that "the collaborative participation of an audience . . . is an integral component of performance as an interactional accomplishment."[7] Auslander quickly dismisses this aspect of Bauman's definition by asserting that it is "very rare that the audience is documented at anything like the same level of detail as the art action. The purpose of most performance art documentation is to make the artist's work available to a larger audience, not to capture the performance as an 'interactional accomplishment.'"[8] However, in the examples provided for this discussion, the audience *is* documented at "the same level of detail" as the performers. In fact, the purpose for recording the "art action" is not to simply document its existence or only to make the artist's work available to a larger audience; the purpose is to record the reactions of the live audience and the interactions between the live audience and performer(s) *for* the audience of the mediatized reproduction. Can these mediatized documents of live performance still be considered performative? It shall become clear, using J. L. Austin's definition of "performative," that the filmed reproductions of Coco Fusco's, Guillermo Gómez-Peña's, and Sacha Baron Cohen's live performances are not merely documentation of the "art actions," but rather performative events in and of themselves.

In order to illustrate how the filmed reproductions are performative, it would be advantageous to analyze the live "art actions" and the artists who created them. Coco Fusco is a Cuban-American interdisciplinary artist and writer. Many of her performances involve the use of multimedia formats including closed-circuit television and live video-stream ing on the Web.[9] Guillermo Gómez-Peña is a performance artist, writer, Macarthur Fellow, and American Book Award winner. His current work focuses on cultural borders using large-scale performance projects.[10] During the live performances of *Two Amerindians Visit . . .*, Fusco and Gómez-Peña were locked in a cage and performed "'traditional tasks,' which ranged from sewing voodoo dolls and lifting weights to watching television and working on a laptop computer." At each location "zoo guards" would answer patrons' questions. On either side of the cage were panels, one outlining the history of human exhibition, the other detailing the history of Guatinau and its people.[11] Throughout the performances, video cameras followed the action of both performers and audience and filmmaker Paula Heredia conducted one-on-one interviews with select audience members, resulting in the 1993 documentary *The Couple in the Cage*.[12]

Sacha Baron Cohen is a comedian, best known for creating three characters: Ali G, a white British youth who thinks he is black; Borat Sagdiyev, an anti-Semitic faux Kazakhstani journalist; and Brüno, a flamboyantly effeminate Austrian fashionista. The comedy behind all three characters lies in interviews and encounters with unsuspecting private citizens in which he uses these characters to reveal sexism, racism, and homophobia among the public. Like Fusco and Gómez-Peña, Baron Cohen uses Western ideas of the Other (the "primitive Other" in Fusco and Gómez-Peña's case and the "non-Western immigrant" in Baron Cohen's case) in order to generate response from the live audience. While many would refer to Baron Cohen as a comedian or actor rather than a performance artist, he is actually accomplishing, with his face-to-face public

Two Amerindians Visit Madrid, 1992 (the title of the performance changed depending on its venue: *Two Amerindians Visit Madrid*, *Chicago*, *Washington, D.C.*, and so on). Photo by Nancy Lytle. Used by permission of Coco Fusco.

interactions, many of the same things that Fusco and Gómez-Peña do in their performance art. Where Fusco and Gómez-Peña lock the Other in a cage, Baron Cohen releases the Other onto the general population with very similar results. The interaction with the performers as Others is the subject of the live "art action," whereas the audience response to the Others is the subject of the filmed documentation of the "art action."[13]

The key element used in the live performances of these artists is parody. The parody in these pieces causes the audience of the live performance to question what their reactions should be. What they are seeing could be interpreted as humorous, but in the given context, should they be laughing? The most obvious form of parody used by these artists is in the satirical creation of the back stories of their characters. As previously mentioned, Fusco and Gómez-Peña used an explanatory panel next to the cage to outline some of the details of their culture, including the "genuine affection for the debris of Western industrialized popular culture" among the Guatinaui people. The panel goes on to describe the male and female "specimens" in great detail, noting that the male "likes spicy foods, burritos, and Diet Coke," and the female "is fond of sandwiches, pad thai, and herb tea . . . [as well as] serving cocktails and massaging her male partner." As if a discussion of the sexual habits of these "primitive" people makes gawking at them less offensive and more scholarly, the panel notes that Smithsonian anthropologists have "observed that the Guatinauis enjoy gender role-playing together after dark, transforming many of their functional objects in the cage into makeshift sex toys by night."[14] In addition to the panel's outline of the cultural habits of the "specimens," the costumes worn by Fusco and Gómez-Peña and the "artifacts" strewn around the cage serve as either a parodic example of what the general population believes a newly discovered culture might look like (face paint, grass skirts, tribal jewelry, etc.) or are so anachronistic that they are laughable (briefcase, boom box, sunglasses, etc.). Even the stories told by Gómez-Peña (for a small fee) were incoherent nonsensical ramblings. According to Diana Taylor, "everything that the audience saw was blatantly theatrical. . . . Fusco and Gómez-Peña parodied Western stereotypes of what 'primitive' people do."[15]

Like Fusco and Gómez-Peña, Baron Cohen uses parody and Western stereotypes (this time of Eastern European and Middle East cultures) in the creation of his character's back story. The nature of his performance forces him to stay in character for up to eight hours at a time, and unlike the Other presented by Fusco and Gómez-Peña, Borat speaks English. This requires him to have an elaborate back story in order to keep up the charade. He tells of his mentally disabled, caged brother who is sexually taunted by his sister; he is shocked that women are allowed to vote, but horses are not; he is terrified of Jews because he thinks they are behind the attacks of 9/11 but also because he believes they can shift their shapes into cockroaches.[16] He also uses parody in his embodiment of the role to reinforce stereotypes; in a January 2007 interview on National Public Radio (NPR), Baron Cohen says, "I never wash the suit. So when I come into the room, there's immediately this terrible smell. Borat doesn't wear deodorant. So there is this kind of dreadful Soviet-bloc smell the moment I walk in."[17] Just as Gómez-Peña uses nonsensical gibberish, Borat does not actually speak the Kazakh language. Instead, Baron Cohen uses a bizarre hybrid of Polish and Hebrew when speaking in Borat's "native" tongue. It becomes clear that for Fusco and Gómez-Peña as well as Baron Cohen, the act of parodying the culture their characters are from is an essential aspect of the live performances. However, the purpose of recording the live performance is not to provide opportunity to ridicule the Others; in fact, it's the exact opposite. It is the revelatory audience reactions to the parodies created by the artists in the live performances that are the purpose behind their art. The most significant aspect of their performances is not in the live "art action," but in the reaction of the live audiences as captured for our view by the film or video camera.

In addition to revealing negative aspects of Western society, the most common reaction of the live audience presented in the mediatized versions is the desire of the general public to help or teach the Other presented by the performers. During the course of the film, Borat attends a dinner party at the Magnolia Mansion Dining Society somewhere in the Deep South. After offending the hostess by telling her that men in his country would find her unattractive, he asks to be excused to the rest room. While he is gone, his hostess notes, "I think the cultural differences are vast. I think he is a delightful man. It wouldn't take very much time for him to become Americanized." Borat returns to the table with a bag of his own feces (apparently the custom in his fictionalized Kazakhstan). Our hostess is not upset; instead she takes Borat back to the bathroom to "teach" him the way Americans use the toilet.[18] For Fusco and Gómez-Peña, the caged nature of the performance prohibited a lot of opportunities for the audience to "teach" the Other. However, in the one-on-one interviews conducted by filmmaker Paula Heredia, several audience members worry about the morality of confining the "primitives" with questions about when they use the bathroom, if they are getting paid to appear, and whether they "enjoy" being in the cage.[19] These examples reveal to the audience of the mediatized reproductions a kind of cultural superiority among the audience of the live performances. The performers have constructed bizarrely heightened (parodic) Western visions of what Others are. Instead of realizing that the depictions are grossly exaggerated, many in the audience of the live performances believe their role is to help the Other by making them more Westernized. The audience of the reproductions knows what is happening and hopefully understands what the desire to change the Other says about our society in general.

It is interesting to note here that none of the artists fully anticipated the reaction of the live audience during the creation of their performances. In her article on her experiences working on the piece, Fusco admits that she and Gómez-Peña were surprised by the reaction of their audiences: "We had to confront two unexpected realities in the course of developing this piece: 1) a substantial portion of the public believed that our fictional identities are real ones; and 2) a substantial number of intellectuals, artists, and cultural bureaucrats have sought to deflect attention from the substance of the experiment to . . . in their words, our 'misinforming the public' about who we are."[20] Baron Cohen may not have been criticized by "intellectuals" and "cultural bureaucrats," but the act of "misinforming the public" did not go unpunished. Robert Saunders cites no fewer than twelve lawsuits against Baron Cohen and his production company by "supporting actors" in his film who felt duped by Baron Cohen into believing that Borat was real.[21] In another similarity to the response received by Fusco and Gómez-Peña, Baron Cohen admits, in an interview with Terry Gross on NPR's *Fresh Air*, that he was initially surprised by the fact that the public believed his characters were actually real people. In the interview, he goes on to discuss his realization that he could use the fact that people believed his character was real to get them to expose things about themselves. For some reason, this misogynistic, racist, homophobic foreigner makes people comfortable enough to open up. For Baron Cohen, "it's fascinating to see how people are going to react . . . whether people are going to answer with integrity or whether they're going to, you know, reveal certain prejudices that they have."[22] It is the unanticipated reactions of the live audience that make the filmed documentation so compelling and create the performative aspects of the mediatized reproductions.

For these artists the key to eliciting this unexpected reaction is the element of surprise. Unlike Baron Cohen who is able to surprise his live audience with random encounters on the street or preplanned interviews with unsuspecting locals, Fusco and Gómez-Peña use surprise to bring their unsuspecting audience to the event. There was almost no advance publicity for any of the performances, in order to stun the audience and force them to decide for themselves how they felt about what they were witnessing. A flyer created to look like the front page of a supermarket tabloid was used to market the event, thus continuing the parodic aspects of the performance, but without explicitly informing potential audiences that what they would be seeing was, in fact, a performance. According to Fusco, "when an audience knows who you are when you pose the question, they give you a very different answer than when they inadvertently bump into you and have to figure out what is going on."[23]

How do the use of parody, misinforming (or under-informing) the public, and the unanticipated reactions of the live audience transform the mediatized reproductions from mere documentation to performative events in and of themselves? By focusing on the live audience, the filmed reproductions open up avenues of reception for the audience of the mediatized versions that are unavailable to the live audience. According to Diana Taylor, in her commentary on *The Couple in the Cage* (comments that are equally applicable to *Borat*), there are actually two different performative acts occurring in the work. The first is the live interaction between performer(s) and audience; secondly, in filming the live interactions, the transgressive nature of performance is exposed, turning the audience of the first, into the performers of the second. In viewing the mediatized versions of these performances we enjoy seeing the audience (now performers) making fools of themselves. Taylor admits that she feels "very empowered knowing that I 'get it' and 'they' don't," but she also admits that she is bothered by her pleasure: "is this the 'appropriate' response to a history of dehumanizing colonial subjects?"[24] Questions like this continue the performative aspects of the live performance to the mediatized documentation. According to Robert Saunders, "*Borat* [tells] us something about the life and times of the global village in which we live. Often we don't like what we hear or see. . . . [Baron Cohen] has been called a squirmist because he makes us uncomfortable. Our distress stems from the political questions he raises."[25] In watching the reproduction of the live performance, the viewer is forced to acknowledge and hopefully question aspects of his or her self and society that the audience in the live performance may not. The live audience is focused on determining what is real in the performance or how they should react to the parodic aspects of the performance. The exponentially increased number of viewers of the mediatized production know what is real and what is parody; they have not been misinformed by the performers. They can then turn their attention to the larger issues of bigotry, colonialism, and cultural superiority the live performances illustrate.

It is important to acknowledge here that despite the clear parallels between the live and mediatized versions, the ways in which the projects were mediatized and the reason behind their mediatization are very different. While both projects were structured and intended to be reproduced from the onset, Sacha Baron Cohen's live interactions were filmed in order to create a mainstream movie with mass appeal. The live interactions between Baron Cohen and the general public can be considered performance, especially following Bauman's definition of performance (there is no denying the "collaborative participation of the audience"), but the filmed documentation falls into what Auslander refers to as the "theatrical category," involving cases "in which performances were staged solely to be photographed or filmed." Coco Fusco and Guillermo Gómez-Peña, on the other hand, documented their live performances to be shown, presumably, at independent film festivals, in museums, and in the halls of academia, thus falling under the category of "documentary" in Auslander's discussion of performance documentation. Does this distinction affect the performativity of the reproductions? Auslander notes that the two categories are not mutually exclusive, and indeed, there are elements of *The Couple in the Cage* that fall under the theatrical category, such as the one-on-one interviews with select audience members, just as the argument could be made that on some level, *Borat* is documentary in that it provides a record that the live performance actually occurred. For Auslander, "the only significant difference between the documentary and theatrical modes of performance documentation is ideological."[26] The purpose behind the mediatization in no way affects its performativity.

Returning now to J. L. Austin's original theory of performativity, do the filmed reproductions remain performatives? If, according to Austin, a performative is an utterance that is "doing" something, what are these performance documents "doing"? The answer seems clear: the filmed documentations redouble the transgressive nature of performance by allowing the audience of the filmed reproductions to experience both the transgressive "art action" and the transgressive audience response to that "art action." In the case of *The Couple in the Cage* and *Borat*, as Auslander suggests, "the crucial relationship is not the one between the document and the performance but the one between the document and its audience."[27] By engaging the audience of the reproduction in a different way and providing the opportunity for the audience of the mediatized documentation to experience aspects of the live performance unavailable to the original audience, the filmed reproduction, therefore, is performative.

Notes

1. The title of *Two Amerindians Visit* . . . was adjusted for each place of performance. For example, it was presented in Madrid as *Two Amerindians visit Madrid.* The work is also sometimes referred to as *Two Amerindians Visit the West.*

2. *The Couple in the Cage*, VHS, directed by Coco Fusco and Paula Heredia (Chicago: Authentic Documentary Productions, 1993).

3. *Borat: Cultural Learnings of America for Make Benefit Glorious Nation of Kazakhstan*, DVD, directed by Larry Charles (Beverly Hills, CA: 20th Century Fox, 2006).

4. Philip Auslander, "The Performativity of Performance Documentation," *PAJ: A Journal of Performance and Art* 28, no. 3 (September 2006): 1–10.

5. J. L. Austin, "How to Do Things with Words: Lecture II," in *The Performance Studies Reader*, ed. Henry Bial (London: Routledge, 2004), 147.

6. Auslander, "Performativity of Performance Documentation," 5.

7. Richard Bauman, *A World of Others' Words: Cross-Cultural Perspectives on Intertextuality* (Malden, MA: Blackwell, 2004), 9.

8. Auslander, "Performativity of Performance Documentation," 6.

9. "CV/Bio, Coco Fusco," http://www.thing.net/~cocofusco/cv.htm.

10. "Gómez-Peña's La Pocha Nostra," http://pochanostra.com.

11. Coco Fusco, "The Other History of Intercultural Performance," *Drama Review* 42, no. 4 (Winter 1994): 145.

12. *Couple in the Cage,* VHS.
13. Robert A. Saunders, *The Many Faces of Sacha Baron Cohen: Politics, Parody, and the Battle over Borat* (Lanham, MD: Lexington Books, 2008), 33.
14. Fusco, "Other History," 164–65.
15. Diana Taylor, "A Savage Performance: Guillermo Gómez-Peña and Coco Fusco's 'Couple in the Cage,'" *TDR* 42, no. 2 (Summer 1998): 167.
16. *Borat,* DVD.
17. Sacha Baron Cohen, interviewed by Luke Burbank, *Day to Day,* National Public Radio, January 12, 2007.
18. *Borat,* DVD.
19. *Couple in the Cage,* VHS.
20. Fusco, "Other History," 143.
21. Saunders, *Many Faces of Sacha Baron Cohen,* 135.
22. Sacha Baron Cohen, interviewed by Terry Gross, *Fresh Air,* National Public Radio, January 7, 2007.
23. Coco Fusco, "Fusco Responds to Taylor and Kirshenblatt-Gimblett," *TDR* 42, no. 4 (Winter 1998): 11.
24. Taylor, "Savage Performance," 170.
25. Saunders, *Many Faces of Sacha Baron Cohen,* 167.
26. Auslander, "Performativity of Performance Documentation," 1–4.
27. Ibid., 9.

Play-within-a-Play or Theatre-in-Film?

Ingmar Bergman's *Through a Glass Darkly*

Lawrence D. Smith

EARLY IN Ingmar Bergman's 1961 film *Through a Glass Darkly* (*Såsom i en spegel*), the four characters gather for an outdoor performance of a play. The father, David, an established author, is the sole audience member to an original play composed by his adolescent son, Minus. Minus and his elder sister, Karin, perform the short piece for their father, while Karin's husband, Martin, serves as an onstage interlocutor, accompanist, and prompter. The play is entitled *The Artistic Haunting; or, The Tomb of Illusions,* and is about a young man with artistic ambitions who promises undying love to the ghost of a Castilian princess, but he balks at accompanying her to the afterlife and instead abandons her to the tomb. It begins in a conflation of Elizabethan and Romantic styles (Martin tells David: "It is almost like Shakespeare"), and concludes in ironical Modernism, as the would-be artist contemplates turning his encounter into an opera, poem, or painting: "Although the ending has to take a more heroic turn. Let's see: 'Oblivion shall own me and only death shall love me.' That's not bad." This is a parting gibe intended by Minus for his father, a self-absorbed novelist and a distant parent.

Karin's performance as the Castilian princess provides us with a first glimpse into her capacity for mimesis. This ability proves to be inseparable from her powers of religious belief, from her relationships with the three men in her family, from her position as a woman in the world, and from her inner life. Karin, played by Harriet Andersson, seems luminous in her role as the princess from beyond the grave; of all the participants in the performance, she alone seems to live within the play, to be a part of its creation, to be at home within its fiction. In the course of the film's action, we also see Karin in her roles as a sister, as a daughter, and as a married woman. Karin can play all of these roles convincingly, at times, but they weigh on her, they seem imposed from without, she suffers in her effort to exist within the boundaries of these roles and at the same time to sustain a single persona, and she finds that she can no longer continue to shift between these various roles or the realms in which they are performed. Ultimately, Karin deliberately and self-consciously chooses to live within that subjective reality that best suits her, the one that seems to her most real and sustainable. *The Artistic Haunting; or, The Tomb of Illusions* proves, by the end of the film, to have been a metaphor encapsulating Karin's place in the world, as well as the relationships of each of the male characters to Karin's illness: in short, an existential reduction.[1]

Thus, questions concerning the human capacity for mimesis and the tensions between ideas of a divine realm that is imminent, a reality that is discovered, and an imaginary world created through human agency, are fundamental to *Through a Glass Darkly.* In many respects, the film borrows from and includes elements of theatre within itself, opening up another set of questions in addition to those concerning God, illusion, and the everyday: namely, questions of artistic boundaries, interpenetration, and synthesis between the two media of theatre and film. In order to explore such tensions, Bergman makes use of the familiar theatrical convention of a play-within-a-play. The play-within has been in use since the sixteenth century in modern Western drama, and this particular instance provokes associations with a similar scene in *The Seagull* (1896), by Anton Chekhov, in which another aspiring young playwright stages an original work in an outdoor performance for his mother, a celebrated actress, and her consort, a famous author. Here, however, we have a play-within-a-film, albeit a film that the director considered a *kammerspiel,* or chamber play, after the dramaturgical model of August Strindberg.[2] *Through a Glass Darkly* is an intimate drama: four characters in a summerhouse and its environs, undergoing a collective crisis within a twenty-four-hour time span. As has been noted, "Bergman's practice forms an eminent, if not unique, example of a transgressional aesthetic project" in which the conventions and practices of theatre (stage plays, opera, vaudeville, puppetry, ballet, etc.) and filmed drama frequently inform and shape the other.[3]

In this paper, I look at some of these aesthetic transgressions in *Through a Glass Darkly,* particularly the conceit of the play-within, and ask what these reveal about the longstanding relations between theatre and film, and the question of identifying theatre-in-film. Ingmar Bergman (1918–2007) had a long career in theatre, film, television, and even radio drama, although he is primarily thought of as a cinematic *auteur*. So, the overt "theatricality" in this example could be attributed merely to the particulars of his career. But, one may find additional examples of a play-within-a-film, or similarly overt performances that function in a manner similar to the play-within, in the work of Bergman's *cineaste* contemporaries, Agnès Varda (b. 1928) and Michelangelo Antonioni (1912–2007). Such events involve the depiction of both performers and spectators, and are typically related to the existential concerns of the protagonist. Bergman's use of this device of a play-within-a-film shows us three things: first, it evidences a historical bridge and interpenetration between theatre and cinema that is ongoing; second, it demonstrates the persistence of a dramaturgical device that seems appropriate to both media; third, it opens up a line of existential inquiry into the choices that one may make concerning the self, others, and the world.

Writing about the convention of the play-within a few years prior to Bergman's film, Robert J. Nelson emphasizes that our pleasure in things imitated is inseparable from imitation itself, and that while there are formal characteristics shared by drama and ritual, the imaginary world of the play "is not discovered, but created."[4] In analyzing the convention of the play-within and its relationship to the play that contains it, Nelson argues that a play's formality in terms of structure, language, and "the indispensable formality" of occasion or event is what distinguishes it for the spectator; furthermore, it is only the offstage spectator, as a witness to a "double action," who defines the play-within.[5] Nelson further stresses that the play-within-a-play is a uniquely modern phenomenon: "Conscious of all doubt, man becomes self-conscious. Not only the meaning of action but the meaning of meaning is examined. . . . The use of this technique *implicates within the work of art* those considerations which usually remain prior and external to the work."[6] Through this implicating, the play-within captures "a history of itself, a record of the scruples and hesitations in the course of its making, sometimes even a defense or definition of the kind to which it belongs or the conventions which it respects."[7] If this is true, what does a play-within-a-film capture? What history or histories does it have to offer, of itself and of the film that contains it? To what "kind" does a play-within-a-film belong and what conventions does it "respect"? Bergman's tenure at Malmö Municipal Theatre from 1952 to 1958, during which he developed "an intrinsically more direct, uncluttered, actor-oriented style" of direction, was fundamental to his career as a film director also.[8] Birgitta Steene identifies four distinct aspects of his work that are emphasized by various critics at this time: the combination of artistic energy and discipline with the interpretive ability to render the text into performance;

a thorough and insightful reading of the text; an "unusual visual and acoustic creativity"; and a gift for working with actors and inducing excellent performances, individually and collectively.[9] This period was capped by the export of his productions of Goethe's *Ur-Faust* to London and Hjalmar Bergman's *The Saga* to Paris, before starting his new position as resident director at the Royal Dramatic Theatre in Stockholm. His directorial debut on the main stage of this national theatre was Anton Chekhov's *The Seagull*, which premiered on January 6, 1961. This was the first time that Bergman had directed a Chekhov play, and expectations were quite high due to Bergman's successes at Malmö Municipal Theatre, as well as his growing international stature as a cinematic *auteur*.[10] Bergman was an artist who "was aware of both the auditory and spatial dimensions of the production of a play" and would frequently "on stage and also on screen, combine a variety of art forms, and in doing so would transgress their traditional borders."[11] Bergman had also begun to employ the device of a stage-upon-a-stage in order to counter the effect of the enormous playing space of the theatre at Malmö and to help focus the audience's attention more exactly. The platform stage, which Bergman saw as "absolutely the archetypal theater, the very oldest form of theater," continued to inform his practice in theatre and film into the 1980s.[12] In fact, this is the type of stage Bergman used to present the play-within in both *The Seagull* and *Through a Glass Darkly*.

Through a Glass Darkly was filmed and subsequently released during the same time period as Bergman's production of *The Seagull*. The film was shot on the island of Fårö and at the film studio, Filmstaden i Råsunda, from July 12 to September 16, 1960.[13] Thus, the shooting schedule of the film preceded the play's rehearsal period and premiere; the production was given forty-two performances as a part of the repertory of the Royal Dramatic Theatre. On the whole, however, *The Seagull* did not fulfill critical expectations, receiving primarily disappointing reviews from the Swedish press, with a few, perhaps exaggeratedly ecstatic reviews written by foreign critics, such as Kenneth Tynan.[14] Bergman himself was unsparing toward his direction in retrospect, saying that the production was "dreadfully unsuccessful, tired and flabby" and that he was "unhappy at the theatre and thought everything was wrong."[15] In contrast, *Through a Glass Darkly* premiered on October 16, 1961, garnering excellent reviews in Sweden and internationally; it received the Academy Award for best foreign film in 1962.

A prominent feature in both works is the play-within, which may be said to serve as a symbolic or metaphysical reduction of the larger drama. Bergman's treatment of the play-within in *The Seagull* elicited specific praise: "The presentation in the park's theater pavilion before the es-

The Seagull, directed by Ingmar Bergman, Royal Dramatic Theatre of Stockholm. Set design by Marik Vos. Featured performers: Christine Schollin and Per Myrberg. Photo courtesy of the Theater Museum of Sweden. Copyright © 1961 by Beata Bergström.

tate's gentry doesn't come off well and isn't very remarkable either. But what glorious images in the shimmering green dusk with the seagull over the lake which, it is true, we do not see but imagine beyond the sticking up behind the wooden pavilion and a pale statue. Never has this celebrated 'nocturne' worked so charmingly as pure stage imagery. . . . What this ingeniously composed spectacle deals with is, of course, nothing but love's impossibility in a world where all are unfortunate in love, and where little Nina will fall into destruction like a seagull."[16] In both Chekhov's play and Bergman's film, the young artist's play is viewed with skepticism by an older, established artist and parent. Both plays-within occur outdoors, at twilight. And in both, a young woman appearing in the early play-within emerges as a tragic protagonist in her own right by the end of the drama proper.

But there are other interesting comparisons: both Chekhov and Bergman may have been critiquing the practices and ambitions of younger contemporaries through these plays-within. Laurence Senelick observes that the aspiring playwright in *The Seagull* "seems unable to find an original play to express his nebulous ideas" and suggests that a source for Chekhov's play-within may have been *Beyond Human Power,* by Norwegian playwright Bjørn Bjørnsen, which Chekhov criticized as having "no meaning because the idea isn't clear. It's impossible to have one's characters perform miracles, when you yourself have no sharply defined conviction as to miracles."[17] Chekhov made this observation shortly before the debut of *The Seagull*. Similarly, in an interview titled "Underground Theatre Is Self-indulgence," printed during the filming for *Through a Glass Darkly*, and in which Bergman talks about his enthusiasm for directing *The Seagull*, Bergman states, "I care very much for young talents and young enterprises. But this business with small theatres is altogether wrong. It trains neither actors nor audiences. None of them get the right perspective on the theatre as art when they sit in each other's laps. Underground theatre is some kind of spiritual masturbation."[18] In this light, for both Chekhov and Bergman, the play-within can be said to serve as a kind of antithesis to the aesthetics of the larger drama, despite its symbolic affinity with the events of that same drama. It thus serves to record historical performance practices that the author of the play proper was critical toward, yet at the same time preserves a trace of such practices within itself.[19]

What is striking about this cinematic play-within is the degree to which the film's protagonist, Karin, is at home in it. She seems radiant in the role of the Castilian princess, who has died in her "thirteenth year in childbirth." But she is also adept within the production on a number of levels, providing a number of offstage effects, such as ringing the bell and imitating a cock's crow. Karin crowds Martin toward stage left, seemingly oblivious to his presence. When Minus goes up on a line, Karin "prompts" the prompter with a kick, and then literally prompts Minus; this is a humorous moment, but interesting also because the duality of the actor's onstage existence is made transparent. Near the end of the play-within, the Castilian princess retires to the interior of her tomb (the gazebo, or *lusthus*, that Minus has converted into a theatre) and waits for the poet to join her. While the poet remains on stage having second thoughts, the princess quietly announces "I am waiting" ("Jag väntar").

These lines, spoken by Karin as she stands looking out a broken window, are exceptional for a number of reasons—per the layout of the *lusthus*, she is at an interior window, stage right, that is never emphasized in any shot other than these medium close-ups. Thus, Karin is playing out of view, ostensibly from "backstage"; we see her still "in character," but no longer from the perspective of David (her father and audience); for that audience, she is an offstage voice. Karin is thus playing privately, as she does later in "real" life, when she is alone in an upstairs room of the house, communicating with invisible voices and awaiting the "entrance" of God. This is a point in the play-within where cinematic privi-

Såsom i en spegel (*Through a Glass Darkly*), directed by Ingmar Bergman. Production design by P. A. Lundgren. Actors: Lars Passgård, Harriet Andersson, and Max von Sydow. Photo courtesy of the Swedish Film Institute Stills Archive. Copyright © 1961 by AB Svensk Filmindustri.

lege is reasserted, following the spatial logic of the *lusthus* (the theatre), but not of classical editing, per se; and in doing so, it demonstrates the link between this play-within and the "real world" of Bergman's cinematic *kammerspiel.* This link is material and formal, not just conceptual; and the conclusion of the play-within demonstrates an interesting aspect of how this link establishes itself within the diegetic "reality" of the film proper.

Following the performance, the characters take up the house lamps that have served as footlights, and proceed back to the house, laughing and chatting about the play and who will perform the after-dinner chores. But this is also a formal procession, noted by Bergman as "the promenade with the oil lanterns" in the director's shooting script.[20] Karin leads the way, still in costume as the Castilian princess with her crown, bearing a lamp; Martin follows bearing the other two lamps, followed by Minus, still in costume, with David, the audience, bringing up the rear. This procession continues, maintained in a long shot that tracks its unbroken movement in a swivel pan, from the stage through the garden to the rear door of the house, through which Karin and Martin enter. This shot is followed by a medium shot with depth of field, with the father in the foreground, Minus in costume in the background, fencing with his player's sword; Karin appears, still in her Castilian princess wardrobe, at the window of her bedroom to say goodnight to her father. Through this procession and as emphasized by this subsequent shot, the play-world has entered into the domestic life of the house. It also takes hold of the home's environs, as Minus runs out of sight in his costume, around the corner of the house, calling out goodnight to all. This is a basic characteristic of the play-within in film: it is a reduction of key elements of the diegesis; it stands out as an attraction in a manner that reinforces the everyday reality of the diegesis, but it also subsequently affects the behaviors of the characters in their "reality"; the elements of performance suffuse the everyday.

Throughout the 1940s and '50s, a considerable amount of critical attention was being paid by scholars from various disciplines, such as Johan Huizinga, Albert Camus, Jean-Paul Sartre, Simone de Beauvoir, J. L. Austin, Ludwig Wittgenstein, and Gaston Bachelard, among others, to the issues of self and performance, the performative aspects of language, and the nature and structure of the social spaces in which these arise, both in life and art. Writing in 1959, two years prior to the release of *Through a Glass Darkly,* Erving Goffman defined the "backstage" of everyday life as a place relative to the "front" of a given performance "where the impression fostered by the performance is knowingly contradicted as a matter of course"; as supporting evidence, Goffman cites Simone de Beauvoir's observation that, "Confronting man, woman is always play-acting."[21] In Karin's case, it seems that while the upstairs room is a place of refuge from the marital and familial drama of the ground floor, it is still a site of performance and she is not out of view, or entirely "backstage." Karin imagines herself before a range of invisible spectators, including God, who usurp the spectatorial roles of her father, husband, and brother. In fact, the one space where she is out of view, or backstage, in any subjective sense is when she seeks refuge in a wrecked fishing vessel; this site becomes a symbolic abyss, a "cellar" in the spatial scheme of the oneiric house of the drama.[22] Here, the consummation promised between the artist and Castilian princess in the play-within of *The Artistic Haunting* is realized as an act of incest between brother and sister.

The play-within and the role of the Castilian princess are invoked for a second time in the screenplay of *Through a Glass Darkly.* Returning from the wrecked ship to the family home, Karin passes through the garden and stops beside the *lusthus.* She sees something in the grass and picks it up; it is the tinsel-paper crown that she wore as the princess in Minus's play, now wet with rain and falling to pieces. She throws it aside and continues on toward the house. She says, "Would Martin like to help me a little with the packing. I'm so awfully tired."[23] This moment was not included in the final print of the film, but it indicates the significance of the play-within in Bergman's conception of Karin and the story as a whole. Furthermore, its placement parallels the structure of events in *The Seagull* in which Nina returns in the last act and views the abandoned stage that she had once played upon from a new perspective: "I went to look at the garden, to see if our stage was still there. And it's standing to this day. I burst into tears for the first time in two years, and I felt relieved, my heart grew lighter. You see, I've stopped crying. And so, now you're a writer. You're a writer, I'm an actress. . . . We've both fallen into the maelstrom."[24] That this moment was cut from the final version of the film is not surprising. In terms of continuity, we have already seen Karin wearing the crown within the house; also, Bergman may simply have curbed what would have been an aesthetic excess. The significant thing, in addition to the structural similarity to Chekhov's play, is that Karin's performance in the play-within clearly bears a relationship to her condition in the world.

In the climax of Bergman's *kammerspiel,* Karin returns for a final time to the room upstairs and, seemingly, encounters her God. Like the play-within, this performance is observed by her father, who stands outside of the door to the room. Her husband assumes a seat "on stage," replicating his role and physical position from the play-within. When he seeks to intervene, Karin maintains her performance while physically pushing him off stage, as in the play-within. When God appears in the form of a spider, Karin becomes hysterical, later explaining that this "spider god" had tried to crawl up inside of her. This motif of penetration and violation is found elsewhere in the film, but from the standpoint of performance, I wish to stress that this is an act of mimesis that we accept without hesitation: no spider is ever seen or mentioned in this sequence, yet we know absolutely that Karin is terrified. This is the product of the actress imagining a spider in the room and the camera recording an actor's make-believe; the spider is no more present or real than God. Dramaturgically, the emergence of the spider is synchronous with the arrival of a medical helicopter; thus, Bergman employs a literal deus ex machina, and to extraordinary effect.

One could attempt to dismiss the presence of the theatrical within Bergman's work as merely a consequence of his career in both media and, thus, an anomaly. Therefore, I would like to present a few brief examples from two contemporaries of Bergman, Agnès Varda and Michelangelo Antonioni. In the work of both, one can find similar dramaturgical structures concerning performance and matters of identity; these serve to demonstrate that Bergman was not alone in his use of theatrical practices within the medium of cinema.

Varda's work, as well as that of other directors in the French New Wave with which she was associated, provides ample case studies for what may be described as an "interart" approach to analyzing filmed performance. Many of the films "play with several strategies of media representations," removing the traditional oppositions of film to theatre, photography to painting, film to literature, and the like, "blurring the established borderlines between the apparatuses."[25] A particularly relevant case is Agnès Varda's *Cléo de 5 à 7* (1962). While awaiting the results of a cancer screening, a female pop singer, Cléo, undergoes a crisis of identity: leaving behind her handlers, she ventures out into the streets of Paris on her own. Varda combines on-location shooting with real time: the action of the film falls between the hours of 5 and 7. In doing so, the neoclassical unities of time, place, and action (as well as a protagonist of high station) are maintained. So, while the medium is film, one can reasonably argue that the film's dramaturgical sensibility derives from the cultural persistence of French neoclassical theatrical practices. Varda began her career, in fact, as an official photographer for the Théâtre National Populaire in Paris from 1951 to 1961.[26]

Cléo de 5 à 7 relies on a firm sense of realism and identification with the protagonist while at the same time questioning the "reality" that shapes that protagonist's identity; but Varda is less concerned with mimesis than with ideas of performance and the performative. Cléo, in addition to being a performer herself (and performing her "self"), is also witness to several different kinds of performances in the course of her journey. These include being surrounded by masked revelers, seeing a short silent film, observing an artist's model, and happening upon two street performances: a frog swallower and a body piercer.

On the one hand, one can regard these street performances as mere "stunts"; but these events are actually closer to the original sense of the "attraction" that Soviet film director and theorist Sergei Eisenstein advocated in one of his early writings on theatre, and thus bear a relation to the play-within phenomenon. Eisenstein's theatrical theory of montage and attraction stressed that "the quality of *attraction* in theatre is the 'fundamental instrument'": "An attraction . . . is any aggressive moment in theatre . . . that subjects the audience to emotional or psychological influence . . . calculated to produce emotional shocks in the spectator in their proper order within the whole. *These shocks provide the only opportunity of perceiving the ideological aspect of what is being shown, the final ideological conclusion.*"[27]

I wish to emphasize the "within" quality of the attraction and how, like the play-within, it functions as a reduction of the key elements of the drama or spectacle, which Eisenstein further describes as a "molecular (i.e. compound) unity of the *effectiveness* of theatre and of *theatre as a whole.*"[28] Film historian Tom Gunning famously adapted the term *attraction* from Eisenstein in order to identify a historical "cinema of attractions" prior to the development of narrative film in the mid-1910s. Gunning uses the term to describe the popular appeal of early cinema as a technological novelty in itself and as a vehicle for exhibiting brief, spectacular events independent of any narrative. But while Gunning's historical analysis is sound, his employment of Eisenstein's idea of "attraction" to describe filmed novelties with no relation to narrative (that is, theatre) seems inaccurate.[29] Rather, Eisenstein stressed that the attraction "has nothing in common with the stunt" or trick, because of the quality of absolute self-containment belonging to the stunt, whereas the attraction "is based on something relative, the reaction of the audience."[30] While both the attraction and the stunt are overt modes of performance, the attraction functions as a distillation of the events and ideas of the larger drama; Eisenstein's "reaction" relies on the same engagement of the spectator that Nelson later identified as necessary for the play-within to achieve its distinction. This quality seems inherent, even primordial, to the phenomenon of performance: it engages and is conspicuous at the same time. This fact was not lost on Bergman: "The real theater always reminds—the real theatrical experience always must remind the audience that it is watching a performance. . . . Because the function of the spectator—if we talk about *an ideal spectator watching the ideal performance*—is that he continually undergoes changes of mind, changes in his concentration. . . . The spectator is always involved and he is always outside, at one and the same time."[31]

So, what does this accomplish when a play-within, an attraction, or some other overt mode of performance is represented within a film? In the case of *Cléo de 5 à 7*, the audience is both on screen and seated in the house. Cléo, who as a performer and a woman has been the object of the gaze in the earlier portion of the film, is now the spectator; yet these performances that she witnesses, and feels revulsion toward, also offer potential information to and about her. Bulimia and self-mutilation are the foundational practices underlying these performances; both are directly linked to the career ambitions of (male) performers for the benefit of a popular audience. Their inclusion in the film hints at modes of self-abuse that might accompany Cléo's celebrity, and may be symbolical extensions to the character's cancer on the level of metaphor.

But, these two attractions also demonstrate the malleability of the body, however grotesquely, via the action of performance; and the protagonist takes up this potential for herself in an act of solitary play. In a later sequence, Cléo performs alone, like Karin in the empty upstairs room in *Through a Glass Darkly*. She improvises a follies staircase number on a flight of steps in Parc Montsouris and, reaching the bottom of the stairs, drops the "act" in order to resume her solitary sojourn. Again, the performance stands in contrast with the everyday; but, in being undertaken by the protagonist, this "performance-within" provides the protagonist with an alternative to her habitual modes of existence (including previous kinds of performances that she has given). In her act as a follies dancer, Cléo seems to have genuine fun and expresses in an extraordinary physical fashion the experience of freedom that she has achieved through her walk alone. Dropping the act, Cléo seems more "real" to us and herself; she walks rather than dances, and continues along her way. The overt performance will affect the subsequent action of the drama.[32]

An additional supporting example is found in Michelangelo Antonioni's *L'avventura* (1960). In this film, there is no play-within, nor are there any attractions or otherwise overt performances; but the female protagonist, Claudia, still engages in various forms of mimesis and private "play." Like *Through a Glass Darkly* and *Cléo de 5 à 7*, *L'avventura* is concerned with identity, specifically with a search for identity on the part of a female protagonist, and the attendant question of surrogate or mimetic role-playing. Claudia experiments with elements of costume and wigs, and engages in a brief episode of play, making faces before a mirror during an evening of anxiety and insomnia. It is worth noting that this event evokes comparison with another bit of foolery before a "mirror" in the Marx Brothers vehicle *Duck Soup* (directed by Leo McCarey in 1933), which in itself is an example of an "interart" approach in which the cinema subordinates itself to a performance deriving from vaudeville. As slight as this example may seem, this event of a character-at-play still functions in the same manner and achieves a similar effect as the similarly overt performances of the play-within in *Through a Glass Darkly* and the attractions in *Cléo de 5 à 7*. In this case, Claudia performs for herself via a mirror; she is simultaneously both actor and spectator.

Cléo de 5 à 7, directed by Agnès Varda. Actor: Corinne Marchand. Photo courtesy of the Swedish Film Institute Stills Archive. Copyright © 1962 by Ciné-Tamaris.

And in Antonioni's film, as with Karin in the play-within and Cléo on the park steps, when the protagonist's "performance" is concluded, the "reality" of that character's life and, by extension, the diegesis as a whole is reasserted for the spectator, intensifying the effect of the verisimilar plot and acting. This small, sublimated performance in *L'avventura* thus poses the same question as the attractions in *Cléo de 5 à 7* and the play-within in *Through a Glass Darkly:* it is used to challenge the everyday by providing an alternative through performance.

In all three films, these performances indicate the element of choice in constructing identity, specifically with respect to their female protagonists. But they also demonstrate a fundamental distinction that we make between "performance" and the "everyday": the performance stands out; it is conspicuous and short-lived, a contrast to "reality." The performance is never typical, but always exceptional. The play-within captures something basic about its container. The attraction does the same thing; both stand distinctly as an extraordinary event that captures and discloses something basic about both the enacted drama and the means through which the drama is delivered, what I consider a separate register of performance. The irony, of course, is that such phenomena should emerge within a greater performance that seeks, in most cases, to represent a dramatic narrative that is also plausible and therefore acceptable as "real" to its audience. In this respect, it is curious that a performance- or play-within should appear at all within a verisimilar play or film. In terms of this ability to include other performances within itself, the performance tradition that narrative cinema seems to have the greatest similarities with is theatre. Yet, these two media seem to have a troubled relationship, and theatre and cinema scholarship maintain a substantial distance from one another despite the fact that there is clear interpenetration of the two media historically, and that both rely, in most instances, upon actors playing characters, or human beings pretending to be other human beings.

French film director and critic Jean-Luc Godard, who was both an advocate for Bergman and one of Varda's contemporaries in the French New Wave, aptly described the process of shooting a film as *théâtre verité:* "I see no difference between the theater and movies. It is all theater. It is simply a matter of understanding what theater means."[33] Godard's observation (and challenge) is to reconsider what is meant by theatre, as well as to challenge typically held views of cinema as an activity wholly distinct from the theatrical. This distinction has had a long life in terms of film theory and criticism, but its currency in the mid-twentieth century is contemporaneous with questions of identity and performance not only in film and theatre, but also in philosophy, sociology, psychology, and linguistics. A basic distinction that is frequently made between theatre and film is the condition of "live-ness"; the theatre offers an event in the moment, while the cinema provides an event after the fact, something that has been previously recorded, edited, assembled, and so on. But, at some point, there typically *is* a live-action performance that the camera records. Writing in 1951, French critic André Bazin offered the following analysis: "Hence it is no longer as certain as it was that there is no middle stage between presence and absence. It is likewise at the ontological level that the effectiveness of the cinema has its source. It is false to say that the screen is incapable of putting us 'in the presence of' the actor. It does so in the same way as a mirror—one must agree that the mirror relays the presence of the person reflected in it—but it is a mirror with a delayed reflection, the tin foil of which retains the image."[34] While the originary performance at the "ontological level" is in progress, it may still be interrupted, stopped, redone, altered, and such, but in ways more characteristic of a rehearsal situation in a theatrical context. It is still a performance. A fairly straightforward term is used to describe all those elements that are not explicitly photographic: *mise-en-scène,* literally "put on stage." This is an indication that a part of the activity of making a film is, in some sense, theatrical.

This is a part of what I take to be Godard's meaning of "*théâtre verité.*" Theatre and film scholars both tend to overlook the live performance that makes the cinematic performance possible, in most cases, in favor of formal analyses, editing, discussions of absence and presence, "liveness," the "gaze," and a host of other valuable and insightful modes of criticism that, nevertheless, overlook the dependence of these later effects on the rather humble practices of live performance, such as acting, singing, dancing, or even frog swallowing.

One thing that can be said about the play-within and the attraction is that the inclusion of such events is a way to elevate the drama, filmed or staged, by including a register of overt performance.[35] I find that this sleight-of-hand which makes the diegesis "real" while also providing the exhilaration of the non-real or extraordinary (in other words, performance) is a basic value of the play-within. But the persistence of the play-within, the attraction, or even a throwaway action as seemingly innocuous as making faces in a mirror, perhaps reveals something basic about the character of performance itself. Despite the degree of development or formality (the play-within arguably is more aesthetically complex than the street performance of a frog swallower, which in turn is more structured and socially complex than a few moments of making faces before a mirror), these events are all extraordinary in terms of effort; they must be consciously undertaken by the performer(s) and can be maintained only for a certain duration. What seems to be demonstrated is that the nature of performance is limited and circumscribed, that it is an action requiring a unique degree of energy and concentration that affects our (performer and spectator) experience and perception of time and space. As aspects of a larger performance, the play of *The Seagull* or the film of *Through a Glass Darkly* on the whole, events such as a play-within appear as a kind of excess, as if the discreet mode of verisimilar representation sustaining the larger performance required some additional, more conspicuous register of play or signification as a kind of aesthetic release or outlet.

With this in mind, it is worth noting that *Through a Glass Darkly* was recently adapted for the stage and produced at the Almeida Theatre in London. The play-within, here titled *The Artist and Death,* is discussed, but no part of it is presented. Karin says that she has memorized the prologue, but when she tries to recite it for their father at the dinner table, he cuts her off and says that he prefers to read the play later, in its entirety. It is obvious that he does not wish either to hear or to read his

Through a Glass Darkly, directed by Michael Attenborough. Almeida Theatre, London. Set design by Tom Scutt. Actors: Justin Salinger, Ruth Wilson, and Ian McElhinney. Photo courtesy of Simon Annand. Copyright © 2010 by Simon Annand.

son's play.[36] The play-within is aborted, as it were, and the emphasis is on the father's rejection of his son rather than the social performances that maintain the family, Karin's gift for mimesis, and the questions of play-acting and faith.

In fact, there was no aesthetic need for overt theatricality within the Almeida production, for there was no illusion of scenic realism to augment or contrast with a "theatrical" construction such as the play-within. The set, designed by Tom Scutt, was based on the idea of spatial flexibility at work within the basic elements of the house: stone and wood. The overall effect of the setting was consistently monolithic, but walls could shift and swivel, hidden panels could open in stone walls revealing cupboard spaces, a trapdoor allowed a bed to appear and disappear, and a continuous line, evocative of both a sea horizon and mildew, sustained an effect of being both inside and outside simultaneously.[37] In short, the physical setting was versatile and evocative, a descendent of the modernist designs of Craig and Appia and the New Stagecraft. Realism was the burden of the actors. And the approach was, in fact, one of acute psychological realism: a portrait of the advancement of Karin's mental illness, surrounded by the shifting scenographic apparatus of the theatre.

There was no question of the possibility of God, and no need for conspicuous play-acting. Thus, the psychological realism dispensed with any metaphysical questions, and the overt theatricality of the set made the performance of a play-within redundant.[38]

One may look at the phenomena of the play-within, the attraction, or the character-at-play in a number of ways, but generally within a spectrum positioning this kind of event, at one end, as a meta-theatrical device designed to expose the artifice of the entire performance, and at the other end, as the innermost dimension of the play as a whole. In the former case, the play-within can be considered a deictic reminder of the medium it is found within, a reflexive pointing-to or pointing-out performance conventions. In the latter case, the play-within-a-play has been compared with the unconscious phenomenon of a dream-within-a-dream: "When a particular incident is represented by the dream-work in a 'dream,' it signifies the strongest confirmation of the reality of the incident, the most emphatic *affirmation* of it."[39] But, the play-within, like the attraction, is an event that is experienced; it is neither merely conceptual (an indication of the meta-theatrical or meta-cinematic), nor purely symbolic (static), but is a performative action emerging out of seemingly concrete circumstances. Thus, the persistence of the play-within and other such related phenomena and their manifest presence in so many films indicates a value that we apparently place on overt performances as an exception to the "everyday" that we routinely accept as "reality." The play-within can perpetuate the illusion of the larger drama, demonstrate or offer alternative choices in action, and affect or even infiltrate subsequent actions on the part of characters within the proper plot of the diegesis. Through a curious effect, this register of performance makes conspicuous the expertise of a performer in its physical, immediate, and, when taken up within a film, even media-resistant qualities. Thus, this kind of performance is a window—a window onto the origins of performed drama, in general, a window onto a surprisingly persistent link between the media of theatre and film, and a window into human agency. In the case studies examined above, it serves as an existential demonstration: an affirmative gesture that contests the everyday, thereby disclosing different potentials for being in the world for both performer and spectator.

Notes

The author wishes to thank the Swedish Institute, the Ingmar Bergman Foundation Archives, the Swedish Film Institute Stills Archive, the Theater Museum of Sweden, Margareta Nördstrom, Hèléne Dahl, Ola Törjas, Krister Collin, Marianne Seid, and Svensk Filmindustri, as well as the Almeida Theatre, Stephanie Bell, and Simon Annand. A special thanks to Anna Westerståhl Stenport.

1. Ingmar Bergman, *En filmtrilogi* (Stockholm: P. A. Norstedt & Söners Förlag, 1963), 3. Bergman announces that *Through a Glass Darkly* and the two subsequent films "deal with a reduction" ("Dessa tre filmer handlar om en reducering"). In the subsequent English translation, this was amended to read, "The theme of these three films is a 'reduction'—in the metaphysical sense of that word"; see *Three Films by Ingmar Bergman,* trans. Paul Britten Austin (New York: Grove Press, 1963), 7.

2. Strindberg derived the term from Max Reinhardt's Kammerspielhaus next to the Deutsches Theater in Berlin. See August Strindberg, "Memorandum to the Members of the Intimate Theater (1908)," in *The Strindberg Reader,* trans. and ed. Arvid Paulson (New York: Phaedra, 1968), 67.

3. Maaret Koskinen, "Out of the Past: *Saraband* and the Ingmar Bergman Archive," in *Ingmar Bergman Revisited: Performance, Cinema and the Arts,* ed. Maaret Koskinen (London: Wallflower Press, 2008), 20.

4. Robert J. Nelson, *Play within a Play: The Dramatist's Conception of His Art: Shakespeare to Anouilh* (New Haven, CT: Yale University Press, 1958), 5.

5. Ibid., 6–7.

6. Ibid.; emphasis added.

7. Leslie Fielder, qtd. in Nelson, *Play within a Play,* 10.

8. Frederick J. Marker and Lise-Lone Marker, *The Scandinavian Theatre: A Short History* (Totowa, NJ: Rowman and Littlefield, 1975), 266.

9. Birgitta Steene, *Ingmar Bergman: A Reference Guide* (Amsterdam: Amsterdam University Press, 2005), 563.

10. Henrik Sjögren, *Lek och raseri: Ingmar Bergmans teater 1938–2002* (Stockholm: Carlsson Bokförlag, 2002), 231.

11. Birgitta Steene, "A Professional Assessment: The Power of Shadows or How We Study Ingmar Bergman," in Koskinen, ed., *Ingmar Bergman Revisited,* 218.

12. Lise-Lone Marker and Frederick J. Marker, *Ingmar Bergman: A Life in the Theater* (Cambridge: Cambridge University Press, 1992), 24. Bergman adds, "And the actors stand there and then they climb up onto the wagon or the platform or whatever it is—and suddenly they are powerful, magical, mysterious, multidimensional. *And that is immensely fascinating*" (25; emphasis in the original). Marilyn Johns Blackwell offers an interesting study of Bergman's use of beds as "stages"; see "Platforms and Beds: The Sexualization of Space in Ingmar Bergman's Theatre and Film," in Koskinen, ed., *Ingmar Bergman Revisited,* 64–85.

13. Paul Duncan and Bengt Wanselius, eds., *Regi Bergman* (Stockholm: Bokförlaget Max Ström, 2008), 275.

14. Steene, *Ingmar Bergman,* 597.

15. Ingmar Bergman, *Bergman on Bergman: Interviews with Ingmar Bergman by Stig Björkman, Torsten Manns, Jonas Sima,* trans. Paul Britten Austin (New York: Simon and Schuster, 1973), 150.

16. Nils Beyer, "Ingmar Bergmans "MÅSEN," *Stockholms Tidningen,* January 7, 1961: 4; my translation.

17. Laurence Senelick, trans. and ed., *Anton Chekhov's Selected Plays* (New York: W. W. Norton, 2005), 132–33. Senelick is quoting Chekhov from a letter to Aleksei Sergeevich Suvorin, dated June 20, 1896. No additional citation is provided.

18. Qtd. in Steene, *Ingmar Bergman,* 781.

19. There is also an autobiographical portrait that is preserved, as Minus may reasonably be interpreted as a variation on Bergman's younger self. Bergman was an aspiring playwright in his youth, writing a dozen plays in the course of a summer in 1942; Minus claims a similar output (thirteen plays plus an opera) in the film. See Peter Cowie, *Ingmar Bergman: A Critical Biography* (New York: Charles Scribner's Sons, 1982), 12.

20. Ingmar Bergman, *Film L-131 (Såsom i en spegel)* (Stockholm: AB Svensk filmindustri, 1960; Ingmar Bergman Foundation Archives, B: 028), 33.

21. Qtd. in Erving Goffman, *The Presentation of Self in Everyday Life* (New York: Anchor Books, 1959), 112–13.

22. Gaston Bachelard, *The Poetics of Space,* trans. Maria Jolas (Boston: Beacon Press, 1994), 118.

23. Ingmar Bergman, "Såsom i en spegel," in *En filmtrilogi,* 59.

24. Anton Chekhov, *The Seagull,* in *Anton Chekhov's Selected Plays,* trans. and ed. Laurence Senelick (New York: W. W. Norton, 2005), 180.

25. Jürgen E. Müller, "Intermediality: A Plea and Some Theses for a New Approach in Media Studies," in *Interart Poetics: Essays on the Interrelations of the Arts and Media,* ed. Ulla-Britta Lagerroth, Hans Eklund, and Erik Hedling (Amsterdam: Rodopi, 1997), 301–2.

26. Alison Smith, *Agnès Varda* (Manchester, UK: Manchester University Press, 1998), 3.

27. Sergei M. Eisenstein, "The Montage of Attractions," *Writings, 1922–34* (London: Bloomington: BFI Pub.; Indiana University Press, 1988; 1996), 34; emphasis mine.

28. Ibid.; emphasis in the original.

29. See Tom Gunning, "The Cinema of Attractions: Early Film, Its Spectator and the Avant-Garde," in *Early Cinema: Space, Frame, Narrative,* ed. Thomas Elsaesser with Adam Barker (London: British Film Institute, 1990), 56–62. The essay, while otherwise excellent, essentially offers a binary in which exhibition exists in opposition to narrative. Moreover, the essay, as valuable as it is, generally perpetuates the bias against theatre that I find in much cinema scholarship. Gunning avoids any discussion of the theatre practices that gave rise to the term "attraction," and omits mentioning Eisenstein's mentor, Vsevolod E. Meyerhold. Theatre ("legitimate theatre") largely remains allied with narrative and, by extension, with psychological realism, for example: "Film clearly took the legitimate theatre as its model, producing famous players in famous plays. The transformation of filmic discourse that D. W. Griffith typifies bound cinematic signifiers to the narration of stories and the creation of a self-enclosed diegetic universe" (60). The "legitimate theatre" that Gunning describes has its own history, one with many different strands, and "legitimate" could also be considered

a label developed as part of a marketing strategy that masked the degree of economic interdependence within the American entertainment industry in the early twentieth century.

30. Eisenstein, "Montage of Attractions," 34–35.

31. Marker and Marker, *Ingmar Bergman,* 32; emphasis added.

32. The play-within and other kinds of overt performances-within consistently bear a relation to the existential condition of the protagonist. Another aspect of these performances that deserves further consideration is the degree to which these derive from and impact upon the performer playing the character-at-play. Corinne Marchand, who played Cléo, said of this sequence: "It's the dream of any singer . . . I would have loved to be the lead in a revue, with feathers everywhere, descending the stairs. I realized that dream here." As this statement indicates, such performances can have existential implications for the real performer as well as the on-screen or onstage character. See Corinne Marchand, "Interview," *Cléo de 5 à 7,* DVD, directed by Agnès Varda (The Criterion Collection, 2000).

33. Jean-Luc Godard, *Jean-Luc Godard: Interviews,* ed. David Sterritt (Jackson: University Press of Mississippi, 1998), 14.

34. André Bazin, "Theater and Cinema—Part Two," *What Is Cinema?* trans. Hugh Gray, vol. 1 (Berkeley: University of California Press, 2005), 97. Bazin was not arguing for a consideration of the interpenetration between the two media but rather to preserve sharp distinctions between the two, with a sharp critical preference for film over theatre. However, his 1951 essay was written prior to the release of two films that are arguably interartial and successfully so: *A Streetcar Named Desire* (directed by Elia Kazan, 1951) and *Miss Julie* (directed by Alf Sjöberg, 1951). Both began as successful stage productions under the same directors.

35. See Maaret Koskinen, "'Everything Represents, Nothing Is': Some Relations between Ingmar Bergman's Films and Theatre Productions," in *Interart Poetics,* ed. Lagerroth, Eklund, and Hedling, 99–107. Koskinen observes an important contradiction in Bergman's oft-professed concern with total cinematic illusionism: "It is remarkable how often in his films this is turned into a sort of *investigation of the necessary counterpart in the creation of that illusion*—the audience. This acute awareness of an audience is, arguably, the key to Bergman's aesthetics both in theatre and in film" (104; emphasis in the original).

36. Ingmar Bergman, adapted by Jenny Worton, *Through a Glass Darkly* (London: Nick Hern Books, 2010), 26.

37. *Through a Glass Darkly,* by Ingmar Bergman, directed by Michael Attenborough, set design by Tom Scutt, performers Ruth Wilson, Justin Salinger, Ian McElhinney, Dimitri Leonidas, Almeida Theatre, London, July 6, 2010.

38. This is not to say that the performances were not compelling or that the Almeida production was not successful; but the fundamental questions taken up by the film in 1961 seem at variance with the concerns and aesthetics of this production in 2010.

39. Alexander Grinstein, "The Dramatic Device: A Play within a Play," *Journal of the American Psychoanalytic Association* no. 4 (1956): 49; emphasis in the original. Grinstein is quoting Sigmund Freud from *Interpretation of Dreams.*

Montage and Theatricality as Sources of Estrangement

A Tendency in Contemporary Brechtian Cinema

Nenad Jovanovic

ALTHOUGH BRECHT'S interest in cinema was only intermittent, resulting in comparatively few films and critical writings on the medium, he seems referenced with equal frequency in the literatures on theatre and film. The vast range of filmmakers Brecht has been associated with includes figures as diverse as the Brothers Taviani,[1] whose eclectic style is reminiscent of Italian Neorealism, and—somewhat outrageously—the American sexploitation filmmaker Russ Meyer.[2] The mutual disparity between some of the connotations Brecht's name has acquired in film studies has led the critic Jonathan Rosenbaum to conclude that "One of the most abused critical terms we have is 'Brechtian.'"[3] Because of the term's exceptional breadth, what follows will first define it for this paper's purposes, along with the other terms in the title (in the order of their appearance within it). The paper will then proceed to argue, using the examples of Brecht and Slatan Dudow's film *Kuhle Wampe* (1932) and Jean-Marie Straub and Danièle Huillet's *Geschichtsunterricht* (*History Lessons*, 1972) and *Die Antigone des Sophokles in der hölderlinschen Übertragung für die Bühne bearbeitet von Brecht* (*Sophocles' Antigone in Hölderlin's Translation as Reworked for the Stage by Brecht*, 1992), that Brechtian cinema is increasingly abandoning the once privileged technique of montage as a source of estrangement in favor of theatricality. While the relevance for Brecht and Brechtian cinema of montage—both in the term's general and its specifically cinematic sense—has been extensively investigated,[4] the relationship between the technique and theatricality as applied in the mentioned contexts remains to be explored.

The first of the title terms that needs definition is *montage*. Perhaps the most famous appearance of the term in Brecht is in "Notes to the

Opera 'Rise and Fall of the City of Mahagonny'" (1930), the writer's earliest systematic articulation of the Epic Theatre concept.[5] In the table contrasting dramatic and epic theatre, montage—a principle associated with the latter theatrical model—is juxtaposed to growth.[6] As John J. White notes in *Bertolt Brecht's Dramatic Theory,* three pairs of terms that surround the cited one clarify the sense in which "montage" is used in the context:[7]

DRAMATIC THEATRE	EPIC THEATRE
one scene makes another	each scene for itself
linear development	in curves
evolutionary determinism	jumps

All three contrasts pertain to narrative structure, rather than the other codes of a performance, inscribed in the play text or added in the process of staging. Elsewhere in his writings, however, Brecht uses the term "montage" more broadly, to describe the opposition to the classical and Romantic idea of stylistic organicity,[8] which entails art's concealment of artifice through imitating nature's modes of production.[9] Brecht sometimes refers to montage also in relation to realms other than artistic, a possibility suggested by the term's inherent possession in German of such connotations as construction and assemblage.

For Brecht the theatre practitioner, montage allows, first, the subversion of the Aristotelian unities. Instead of aiming for the impression that scene b "naturally" follows from scene a, and scene c from scene b, an epic play juxtaposes scenes, often employing large chronological gaps to emphasize the changes undergone by the characters during the course of the narrative (to give but one example, *Life of Galileo* spans about three decades of the protagonist's life). Brecht's second use of montage stems from his opposition to Wagner's synergistic concept of the *Gesamtkunstwerk* (or the total work of art), which refers to merging of elements of different arts into a seamless whole. Abandoning this ideal, Brecht proposes their relative independence from each other (the principle of separation, or *Prinzip der Trennung*).

In the context of cinema, and particularly in the English-language discourse on the medium, montage is distinguished from editing to suggest the former's divergence from dominant cinema's aim of creating the illusion of continuity of space and time within film scenes, as well as maintaining a sense of spatial and temporal relationships.[10]

A foremost theorist of cinematic montage and one of few filmmakers Brecht admired, Sergei Eisenstein, identifies several strains of the technique, of which intellectual editing is the most complex. Eisenstein defines the concept as "combining shots that are *depictive*, single in meaning, neutral in content—into *intellectual* contexts and series."[11] The theorist uses the example of Japanese ideograms to demonstrate the viability of a cinema whose formal operations would be based on the Hegelian dialectical triad, whereby synthesis arises from the opposition between thesis and antithesis.[12] Among the examples Eisenstein gives of images combined within the ideograms to create new meanings are water and an eye (signifying weeping), a mouth and a bird (signifying singing), and a knife and a heart (signifying sorrow). A relatively rare practical application of the concept of intellectual editing in Eisenstein's cinema is found in *October* (1929), where the image of a bridge, being opened to kill the protesters against the regime of tzarism, is juxtaposed with a still image of an Egyptian pharaoh's mask. The (evasive) suggestion of the regime's obsolescence is realized through the combination of the two consecutive images, which represents not their mere sum, but their sublation (or *Aufhebung*, to use Hegel's original term): a (the image of the bridge) + b (the image of the pharaoh's mask) = c (the idea of the obsolescence of the tzarist regime). The originality of this concept becomes apparent when it is compared with parallel editing, a cinematic technique pioneered in the late 1900s by D. W. Griffith. The Griffithian parallel editing conforms to the formula a + b = ab (for example, the chaser, nearing the prey during the course of a sequence, eventually catches her, thus bringing two parallel narrative lines together).[13] As later will be demonstrated, intellectual montage is employed in Brecht's only feature film as a codirector (with Slatan Dudow), *Kuhle Wampe* (1932). It is this strain of montage that the term in this article's title refers to.

Second, *theatricality*. Thomas Postlewait and Tracy C. Davis observe that the term theatricality is often used interchangeably with a variety of related but distinct concepts—from mimesis to *theatrum mundi*, from ritual behavior to performativity.[14] In the context of cinema, theatricality can—in Jacques Gerstenkorn's categorization—refer to the following: 1) theatricality as it appears in films that explicitly reference theatrical practice (theatre as content); 2) theatricality as it is produced by a film's use of a characteristically theatrical mode (theatre as a form within a form); 3) theatricality as it is achieved through a process the writer calls recycling (*recyclage*), using a distinctly theatrical convention.[15] All three fit the purposes of this paper.

Third, *estrangement*. The term is one of the English renditions of Brecht's *Verfremdung*,[16] the relation of which concept to dialectics Brecht explains by the triadic formula of "*verstehen—nicht verstehen—verstehen:* understanding—not understanding—understanding."[17] The process of estrangement, then, involves a double negation, and is only completed when the understanding of an observable phenomenon by the recipient of an artwork is renewed. A possible confusion about this term stems from the fact that it is also used to translate Shklovsky's related term *ostranenie*, whose penetration into critical discourse predates that of *Verfremdung* by a few years, and which differs from Brecht's own concept mainly in its lack of an overt political aspect. The article, of course, uses the term "estrangement" in the sense of *Verfremdung*.

Fourth, *contemporary*. As used here, the term denotes the period that started with the crisis of European communisms in the early 1970s, and culminated with their demise following the reunification of Germany.

Fifth, *Brechtian*. In the context of this paper, the term means: substantially influenced by Brecht's theory of Epic Theatre, as acknowledged by the filmmakers themselves. Brecht's theory advocates a theatre suitable for our "scientific era," which enables—and calls for—the explanation of human condition not in terms of a higher power and its whims, but in terms of (alterable) social forces. This task demanded a realism different from its traditional form, predicated on "a montage of discourses."[18]

How are Brecht's views of montage—and of epic dramaturgy in general—applied to *Kuhle Wampe*? The film consists of three episodes, separated by montage sequences that show "images of apartment buildings, factories and natural landscapes."[19] Editing is foregrounded as a dominant technique by a scene from the film's second part, set in the film's eponymous tent colony, where the central group of characters—the Bönike family—has moved after being evicted from their Berlin apartment due to unpaid rent. The scene shows Bönike, the father, reading aloud a newspaper article on Mata Hari as his wife is calculating grocery prices. The brief low-angle shots of Mrs. Bönike, of both her and her husband, and of her hand compiling the list, are interspersed with nondiegetic shots of food items with price tags, photographed through a store window. The luxurious life of dancer and courtesan Mata Hari is contrasted to the family's daily monetary struggle.

Kuhle Wampe uses montage not only as an editing technique, but also as a structuring dramaturgical principle applied at each of its three parts and their constituent scenes. The three parts form a hierarchy that can be designated as dialectical. The first part, centering on a laborer who commits suicide after a vain job hunt, represents a possible answer to a manifestation of the crisis of capitalism (suicide as thesis). The second part, where the dead laborer's family moves to Kuhle Wampe, represents another answer (eviction as antithesis). While the first two parts center on the concerns of the individual, the third, showing a leftist sports festi-

Kuhle Wampe, directed by Slatan Dudow and Bertolt Brecht, 1932. Used by permission of Praesens Film.

val, focuses on the collective and is constructed as the only satisfactory answer to the crisis of capitalism established in the film's exposition (the workers' mobilization as synthesis). All formal operations that assist the content's dialecticity can be associated with montage, once the concept is broadened to include the sound-image relationship.

The film was banned immediately after the Nazis' ascent to power, and continued to circulate in West Germany only in the late 1960s.[20] Its rediscovery appears to have contributed to the shift in focus of critical investigations into Brecht and cinema from questions of narrative to those of style. A culmination of this process is evidenced in the Brecht-dedicated issue of the British film journal *Screen.* In the article "Realism and the Cinema: Notes on Some Brechtian Theses," included in the issue, Colin MacCabe hails *Kuhle Wampe* for rejecting the language of dominant cinema. The language—in accord with the principle of self-effacing craftsmanship that dominant cinema borrows from classicism[21]—dematerializes itself to achieve a perfect representation.[22] This influential view of Brecht in relation to cinema has led to frequent equations in film studies of self-reflexivity, Brechtian estrangement, and political progressiveness. The conflation of the two senses of the term "montage" (that pertaining to narrative on the one hand, and that pertaining to style on the other) may be attributed in part to the use of the term by Eisenstein, who is often classified within the same aesthetico-political category as Brecht.[23] In "The Cinematographic Principle," Eisenstein equates montage with conflict, not only between the elements in adjoining shots, but also between the elements *within* the shots: conflict of graphic directions ("*[l]ines—either static or dynamic,*" either actual or implied through the movement of an object in the shot); conflict of scales (the relative size of objects in the shot); conflict of volumes (the absolute size and shape of objects in the shot); conflict of masses ("*[v]olumes filled with various intensities of light*"); and conflict of depths (the positions of objects in the photographed space and in the film frame).[24] Rainer Friedrich's "On Brecht and Eisenstein" exemplifies the methodological move of applying the term "montage" variably to the narrative and style of Brecht's theatre. Exemplifying the term, Friedrich cites within the same paragraph the dualism of the characters Shen Te and Shui Ta in *The Good Person of Szechwan* (an element of the drama's narrative) and the duality between the actor and the role underlying Charles Laughton's performance of Galileo (an element of the theatre production's style) in Joseph Losey's 1947 staging of Brecht's eponymous drama.[25] Confusions of this sort could perhaps be avoided if the term "the principle of separation" were used instead of "montage" in reference to stylistic discontinuities of Brechtian films and theatrical productions. For this principle, too—as Friedrich correctly observes—is a factor of unity, although contrapuntal (as opposed to organic).[26]

The style of dominant cinema has been changing along with the understanding of Brecht in relation to the medium. The 1950s saw the demise of the Hollywood studio system, which coincided with the ascent of television, European art cinema, and American avant-garde film. All three were factors in the style's evolution, the current phase of which David Bordwell considers deserving of a separate name: intensified continuity. The first strategy Bordwell identifies as characteristic of the contemporary Hollywood style is increasingly rapid editing.[27] However, more important for this discussion than the ever-diminishing average shot length of Hollywood films is that the editing patterns currently employed in the industry often blur the spatio-temporal continuum and the causal relationship among shots and scenes. For instance, in Marc Forster's *Quantum of Solace* (2008), a narrative connection is established between the scene of a horse race and the sequence of an interrogation turning into a chase only after the film has crosscut between the two lines of action for a good minute. Put differently, it takes the film a considerable amount of screen time to confirm that the race scenes belong to the diegesis. While the example does not exemplify intellectual editing, it does represent a departure from the classical Hollywood style of crosscutting, which seeks to avoid any kind of confusion in the narrative or in the organization of filmic space and time.

The strategies of intensified continuity, as well as the described editing pattern in *Quantum of Solace*, aim at distorting the everyday perception of reality, at making the familiar strange. But since the content of most Hollywood films fails to question dominant ideologies, the result is an empty spectacle that deadens the viewer's critical capacities, a far cry from what Brecht aimed for by the use of the technique in his own film practice. Adorno, who in *Aesthetic Theory* (1970) allows that all modern art may be called montage if montage is understood as a broad artistic principle identical to construction (as opposed to "organic commingling" of elements), warns that "[t]he principle of montage was conceived as an act against a surreptitiously achieved organic unity; it was meant to shock. Once this shock is neutralized, the assemblage once more becomes merely indifferent material; the technique no longer suffices to trigger communication between the aesthetic and the extra-aesthetic, and its interest dwindles to a cultural-historical curiosity."[28]

Perhaps recognizing that dominant cinema's adoption of montage has robbed the technique of its estranging potential, contemporary Brechtian filmmakers increasingly adopt as sources of *Verfremdung* the objects within the camera's field of view and the sounds within the microphone's range. I will illustrate this observation by comparing *History Lessons* and *Sophocles' Antigone in Hölderlin's Translation as Reworked for the Stage by Brecht* (hereafter abbreviated *Antigone*) by Jean-Marie Straub and Danièle Huillet, a directorial tandem commonly situated in the context of New German Cinema, a loose movement founded in the early 1960s in protest against the aesthetic and economic backwardness of the country's film industry. The two filmmakers worked together from their debut in 1962 with the short *Machorka-Muff* to 2006, the year of Huillet's death. Straub and Huillet refer to Brecht in their films and writings, two of their films are based upon Brecht's texts, and more than one of their techniques corresponds to Brecht's theoretical tenets.

The bulk of *History Lessons*, based on Brecht's unfinished novel *Die Geschäfte des Herrn Julius Caesar* (*The Business Affairs of Mr. Julius-Caesar*, 1938–39), consists of scenes of dialogue between an anonymous young man and representatives of different classes and professions who knew Caesar personally. The dialogue scenes are interspersed with those showing the young man silently driving the streets of Rome. The film produces estranging dialectical dualities by departing from the norms of descriptive realism and pointing to its artifice. First, it combines modern costume for the young man and togas for the other characters, and configures the Rome of the ride scenes as contemporary. The two anachronisms challenge the spatio-temporal continuum a traditional cinematic narrative seeks to maintain, enhancing the novel's parallel between slavery (the dominant social system of Caesar's era) and capitalism (the dominant social system of the young man's era). Another of the film's structural dualities results from the use of languages (verbal and visual) in the dialogue scenes, and their absence from the ride scenes. The verbal language is Brecht's prose; the visual one is that of dominant cinema. More specifically, many of the dialogue scenes rely on a reformulated element of this language, namely the shot-countershot. In the scene with the peasant, the camera performs what Martin Walsh describes as intertwined circling of the two men: the alternating shots from the peasant to the young man fulfill the demands of the shot-countershot, but the camera placements, showing the characters from incompatible angles, do not.[29] The ride scenes, in contrast, use no dialogue and no editing (all three scenes are shot-sequences photographed from a fixed camera position). The third group of the film's dialectical dualities, concerning the mise-en-scène in the ride scenes, will be discussed at some length in the article's next segment.

Shot from the camera fixed in the backseat of the protagonist's convertible, these scenes do not obey the logic of narrative buildup that governs mainstream narrative cinema: none of the micro-events seen in the background of the frames is configured as dominant; none seems more important than the other. The ride scenes, as Walsh observes, serve as an index of the unintelligibility of history,[30] inviting us "to seize moments for analysis, draw knowledge out of chaos: systematize flux, immobilise flow, in order to attempt to comprehend it."[31]

The image of the young man in the car possesses a duality also in terms of action. In the context of the film that—like Brecht—challenges the notion of history as a matter of the past, the character's simultaneous moving and stillness becomes a trope for agency. Riding through the kind of Roman streets never shown on tourist flyers for the city, the young man's role fluctuates between that of a participant in and a mere observer of his surroundings.[32] The car's windshield distances him from the environment, but this distance gets closed by the turning wheels. If the prerequisite for the young man to take political action is to synthesize the information collected from his interviewees and the sights and sounds perceived during the ride, the prerequisite for the viewer to synthesize the film's material can be said to be a perceptual shift that will allow them to accept the ride scenes as action proper, equal in importance with the interviews.

Geschichtsunterricht (*History Lessons*), directed by Jean-Marie Straub and Danièle Huillet, 1972. Used by permission of Jean-Marie Straub.

The film invites a parallelism between the young man and the viewer, but it simultaneously discourages the process of identification promoted by dominant cinema with its Aristotelian roots. The camera shows the young man from the back, its vantage point preventing the viewer's interpretation of the sights and sounds of the streets in terms of his reactions to them. However, the rear-view mirror in front of the character returns his look, calling attention to the film's artifice, to the fact that what the viewer perceives as the character is merely an image, equal in status with the character's reflection in the center of the frame.[33] Showing an object in the manner of Cubist painters, from different directions, appears to mock the very phenomenon of perspective, which the shot otherwise emphasizes through the lines both present within it and only implied. The spatial split beside the direction of the man's look (returned at the viewer) and the direction in which he is moving rhymes with the temporal split indicated by the combination of modern and period costumes, thus connecting the two groups of scenes.

The final dialectical split within the film concerns images (dominant in the ride scenes) and words (dominant in the dialogue scenes). The fact that the impressions expressed in the previous sentence through the adjective "dominant" can be challenged raises pertinent questions: is the viewer's presumed tendency to rely on her hearing for the interview scenes, and on her sight for the ride ones, a sign of perceptual laziness? Would she be able to understand the workings of history better if she mobilized both senses?

History Lessons can be regarded as a paradigmatic montage film not merely because of the duality of its structure, but also for two more reasons: first, it manages—while foregrounding editing—to be dialectical through the use of other formal elements, and second, it conforms to the above formula of intellectual editing even more strictly than Eisenstein's own scenes and *Kuhle Wampe*. While Eisenstein uses the technique only in certain scenes, the juxtaposition of two kinds of material in *History Lessons* that form a dialectical relationship occurs throughout the film. Moreover, while Dudow and Brecht's film offers a synthesis of the dialectical opposition represented by the film's two parts (the episode showing the workers' mobilization through sport), *History Lessons* is resolutely open-ended. The "c" of the above-quoted Eisenstein's formula of intellectual editing is, in the case of this film, not the viewer's idea of the meaning that dialectically overcomes the "a" and "b" (the dialogue scenes and the ride scenes), but the viewer herself. If the progressiveness of a film can be measured by the force with which it compels the viewer to participate in the creation of its meaning—as *Screen* theorists posit is the case—*History Lessons* is worthy of the adjective "progressive." Barton Byg's commentary on Straub and Huillet's *Moses und Aaron* (1974) applies here, too: "A parallel to Straub/Huillet and Brecht emerges here. There is no 'resolution' in their work, according to the hierarchical rules of traditional organization of meaning, but the relation of the organization of its materials to these traditional forms implies a resolution outside the work itself."[34]

Unlike *History Lessons, Antigone* uses a relatively unobtrusive audiovisual style in conjunction with theatrical conventions. It should be noted at the outset of the discussion of this film that the appearance of theatrical conventions in the filmmakers' cinema did not start with *Antigone:* George Lellis, commenting on Jean Narboni's *Cahiers du cinéma* critique of Straub and Huillet's filmic adaptation of Corneille's *Othon* (1969), notes the film's relation to theatre.[35] Narboni's use of the term "theatricality" is, however, crucially different from this article's. The *Cahiers du cinéma* critic introduces the term "theatrical scene" in contrast to linear perspective, which dominant cinema seeks to emulate. *Othon* is, he stresses, independent from the play text, which fact manifests itself in the way the film counters the cinematographic illusionism through frequent editing discontinuities, the presence of random noises of the soundtrack such as horn sounds of the cars riding by the location, and the acting style that emphasizes the abstract aural qualities of the actors' deliveries rather than the words themselves.[36] For these reasons, Lellis concurs with Narboni: *Othon* "exists only for the camera."[37] *Antigone,* in contrast, asserts its palimpsestuous character not only through the title—which invokes all writers who have had a hand in the text—but also through the deliberately maintained traces of the production's initial incarnation as a theatre show produced at Berlin's Schaubühne in 1991. While *History Lessons* challenges the viewer to figure out the relationship between the two kinds of material, this *Antigone* raises questions of its relationship to the previous ones: the play's first performance, Hölderlin's *Antigone,* Brecht's *Antigone,* and Straub and Huillet's own theatrical version of the tragedy, thus blurring the distinction between the original and adaptation as its "copy."[38]

In Brecht's adaptation, the chorus is transformed into the elders financially benefiting from Kreon's war. (Their first line in the adaptation is "The wagons of booty are coming! The victory loaded with plunder to make Thebes forget the war!")[39] The relative complexity of the back story in the original play is done away with, the result being a concentration of the viewer's attention to the mechanism that links capitalism, war, and tyranny, as it is embodied in Kreon. "When I attacked Argos," he says, "who sent me? The metal spears went out / to bring metal from the mountains / at your request; for you know Argos / is rich in metals."[40] Brecht diverts focus from Argos to its exploiter, Thebes, by making Polynices and Eteokles soldiers of the same, Kreon's army. After seeing his brother killed on the battlefield, Polynices runs away to the desert, where Kreon himself punishes him by death.

The variety of angles and shot scales in *Antigone* is achieved solely through the use of lenses with different focal lengths and horizontal movements around the axis. The many camera pans explore the diegetic space freely, while simultaneously keeping, as Byg observes, the taboo of the space where the camera stands.[41] The camera's fixity invokes that of the viewer of traditional film and theatre, consequently implicating them in the narrative. It is as if the Antoinian fourth wall is crossed not by the actors—as happened regularly in Brecht's productions—but by the cinematographic apparatus itself. In other words, the camera hints at its presence precisely by denying the spectator a view of its position within the setting. The identified self-conscious stylistic premise is, however, not overt, but backgrounded. Hence Peter Handke's comparison of the "machinery" the film uses with that of Hawks or Raoul Walsh in the golden era of Hollywood.[42] In terms of the correlation between means and ends, then, *History Lessons* and *Antigone* stand in contrast to one

Danièle Huillet, the actress Libgart Schwarz, and Jean-Marie Straub at the set of *Antigone,* directed by Straub and Huillet, 1992. Used by permission of Jean-Marie Straub.

another: the former film uses a reformulated element of the syntax of dominant cinema to point to its own constructedness, whereas the latter uses an experimental stylistic premise to achieve the impression of a spatio-temporal continuity.

The relative transparence of the film's cinematography—and editing, as a concomitant technique—allows its theatricality in terms of both narrative and style to come to the fore. The first of three elements through which theatricality is achieved is the play text. Straub and Huillet eliminate the Brecht-added prologue to the drama which is set in Berlin in April 1945,[43] thus restoring the Aristotelian unities of the original. The second distinctly theatrical element is the setting: *Antigone* was shot in the Teatro di Segesta, a Greek theatre in Sicily dating from the fourth century BC. The third—and most prominent—theatrical element is the style of delivery and blocking. Characteristically, Straub and Huillet combine actors of various degrees of experience and ability. The figures' movements and gestures are extremely measured and used mostly for emphasis. Kreon, for example, when faced with Hamon's criticism of his rule, asserts his power by swinging his scepter as he dismisses his son's words on the account of his ignorance of the case, and raises his arms high in the air upon receiving the news of Megareus's death. Finally, the actors invariably follow the caesuras of Brecht's verse, pausing at the end of each line.

The pace of the cutting typically follows that of the delivery. When applied to quick exchanges, this logic—as Laurence Giavarini has observed—works to enhance the effect of stychomitia, already created by the dialogue.[44] The film's earliest example of this sort occurs when Kreon asks for the elders' approval to leave Polynices unburied. Their reply—"We approve it"—marks the beginning of a series of seven brief shots, in all but one of which a single sentence line is spoken by the character(s) shown in the image. Shot-reverse shot technique here employed is, of course, used also in continuity editing, the editing style dominant in Hollywood and other mainstream cinemas. But while a mainstream film would smooth the cuts through the use of sound bridges, *Antigone*—like *History Lessons*—rejects this essentially illusionistic device.

The same effect of drawing the viewer's attention to the cinematographic apparatus is achieved by carrying to an extreme the use of offscreen space in the instances where the film refrains from cutting for a relatively long period of time. For example, the camera holds Antigone in close-up for the portion of dialogue that occupies over two pages in the printed version, starting with the protagonist's words to the elders: "And you take it and let him shut you up."[45] Even more overt use of offscreen space occurs in the segments of shots devoid of human figures.

All four of such images in the film (each accompanied with an ode of the elders, and introduced through a pan away from the actors) show a stone formation in the ground that appears to mark the boundary between the orchestra and skene.

The original function of the two architectural elements of ancient Greek theatre seems relevant here. During a performance, skene would be occupied by a temporary construction with double purpose: to represent the location of the drama, and to serve as the changing-room for the actors. By temporarily abandoning the transparency of the film's style through self-conscious camera movements, and pointing to the dividing line between the space in the theatre of Segesta where the actors appeared in character, and the space where they were permitted to step out of it, Straub and Huillet seem to subtly invite the viewer to a meditation on the relationship between representation and presentation, between illusion and reality.

The estranging quality of the performance style in *Antigone* becomes apparent when set against the Stanislavski-inspired acting techniques of mainstream cinema. The dialectics of form (which lies in the contrast between the cinematography and editing and the theatrically stylized acting) mirrors the dialecticity of content. The latter is achieved by emphasizing the palimpsestuous nature of the play text and by giving the film a dialectical-materialist slant via the adaptation.

Examples of different manifestations of theatricality are found also in the recent output of other Brechtian filmmakers whose earlier works rely on montage and other medium-specific cinematic techniques. Consider, for example, the multilayered figure compositions in Peter Watkins's *La commune (Paris, 1871)* (The Commune [Paris, 1871], 2000), and the chalkboard setting in Lars von Trier's *Dogville* (2003) and *Manderlay* (2005).[46] Finally, a caveat: the above discussion does not suggest that montage and theatricality cannot coexist as sources of *Verfremdung*. To paraphrase Brecht's footnote to the dramatic versus Epic Theatre schema: what I have discussed concerns merely a shift in emphasis (albeit a radical one).

Notes

1. Maiia Turovskaia, *Na granitse iskusstv: Brekht i kino* (Moskva: Iskusstvo, 1985), 224–33.

2. Doyle Greene, *Lips Hips Tits Power: The films of Russ Meyer* (London: Creation, 2004), 217.

3. Jonathan Rosenbaum, "*Mother Courage and Her Children* and *History Lessons*," http://www.jonathanrosenbaum.com/?p=6576 (accessed May 6, 2010).

The terminological confusion around the term in the context of film studies is alleviated by Martin Brady's "Brecht and Film" (in Peter Thomson and Glendyr Sacks, eds., *The Cambridge Companion to Brecht* [Cambridge, UK: Cambridge University Press, 2006], 297–317.) Brady identifies three kinds of Brechtian cinema existing at present, each suggestive of one broad meaning of the adjective. Beside Brady's, the following English-language articles on the subject strike a balance between comprehensiveness and concision: Thomas Elsaesser, "From Anti-illusionism to Hyper-realism: Bertolt Brecht and Contemporary Film," in *Re-interpreting Brecht: His Influence on Contemporary Drama and Film*, ed. Pia Kleber and Colin Visser (Cambridge, UK: Cambridge University Press, 1990), 170–85; Marc Silberman, "Brecht and Film," and Barton Byg, "Brecht, New Waves, and Political Modernism in Cinema," in *A Bertolt Brecht Reference Companion*, ed. Siegfried Mews (Westport, CT: Greenwood Press, 1997), 197–219 and 220–37, respectively; and Angela Curran, "Bertolt Brecht," in *The Routledge Companion to Philosophy and Film*, ed. Paisley Livingstone and Carl Plantinga (London: Routledge, 2009), 323–32.

4. See, for example, Roswitha Mueller's *Bertolt Brecht and the Theory of Media* (Lincoln: University of Nebraska Press, 1989), 67–95.

5. In his later theoretical writings, Brecht refers to a somewhat evolved version of the theatrical model presented in "Notes" as dialectic. To highlight the focus of my inquiry on the similarities, rather than differences, between Brecht's different articulations of the concept, I use both terms in reference to it.

6. The translation of this, and the terms from the below-quoted section of Brecht's epic/dramatic theatre table, is borrowed from Bertolt Brecht's *Brecht on Theatre*, ed. and trans. John Willett (London: Methuen, 1964), 37.

7. John J. White, *Bertolt Brecht's Dramatic Theory* (Rochester, NY: Camden House, 2004), 56.

8. Rainer Friedrich, "On Brecht and Eisenstein," *Telos* 31 (Spring 1977): 156.

9. Brecht's anti-Kantian stance, investigated by Jan Bruck in relation to the concept of realism in the writer's "Brecht's and Kluge's Aesthetic of Realism" reflects itself also in the antagonism Brecht shows against Kant's dictum from *Critique of Aesthetic Judgment* that "the finality in the product of fine art, intentional though it be, must not have the appearance of being intentional, i.e., fine art must be capable of being viewed as nature, is by the presence of perfect exactness in the agreement with rules prescribing how alone the product can be what it is intended to be, but with an absence of labored effect . . . i.e., without a trace of the artist having always had the rule presented to him and of its having fettered his mental powers." Jan Bruck, "Brecht's and Kluge's Aesthetic of Realism" in *Poetics* 17, no. 1–2 [1988]: 57–68; and Immanuel Kant, qtd. in Rainer Friedrich, "On Brecht and Eisenstein," 156. In his discussion of the idea of art's imitating nature's modes of production, Robert E. Wood traces the idea back to Plotinus. Robert E. Wood, *Placing Aesthetics: Reflections on the Philosophic Tradition* (Athens, OH: Ohio University Press), 308.

10. The term "dominant cinema" is used to denote major film industries, all of which conform, in slightly varying degrees, to the narrative and stylistic principles of Hollywood.

11. Sergei Eisenstein, *Film Form: Essays in Film Theory,* ed. and trans. Jay Leyda (San Diego: Harcourt Brace Jovanovich, 1977), 30.

12. Ibid., 45.

13. Note that if the variables a and b are broadened to apply not only to characters, but also to objects and abstractions, the simple formula becomes applicable to the dramaturgy of all mainstream, goal-oriented cinema.

14. Thomas Postlewait and Tracy C. Davis, "Theatricality: An Introduction," in *Theatricality,* ed. Tracy C. Davis and Thomas Postlewait (Cambridge, UK: Cambridge University Press, 2003), 33.

15. Jacques Gerstenkorn, "Lever de rideau," in *Cinéma et Théatralité,* ed. Christine Hamon-Sirejols, Jacques Gerstenkorn, and André Gardies (Lyon: Aléas, 1994).

16. The other, equally common ones are alienation, distanciation, and defamiliarization.

17. Bertolt Brecht, *Gesammelte Werke in 20 Bänden* (Frankfurt am Main: Suhrkamp Verlag, 1967), 15:360.

18. Peter Wollen, "Manet: Modernism and Avant-Garde," *Screen* 21, no. 2 (1980): 23. Wollen offers a useful summary of why Brecht considered a traditional form of realism inadequate for what he considered the task of modern art: "On a purely descriptive level it tended to be local rather than global, and to show what was present simultaneously rather than past and future. It favored the actual rather than the possible and the observable rather than the unobservable. It was descriptive rather than explanatory. It effaced contradiction" (23).

19. Bertolt Brecht, "The Sound Film *Kuhle Wampe* or *Who Owns the World*? in *Brecht on Film and Radio,* ed. and trans. Marc Silberman (London: Methuen, 2000), 205.

20. Marc Silberman, "Whose Revolution? The Subject of *Kuhle Wampe,*" in Noah Isenberg, ed., *Weimar Cinema: An Essential Guide to Classic Films of the Era* (New York: Columbia University Press, 2009), 311.

21. In *The Classical Hollywood Cinema* (London: Routledge and Kegan Paul, 1985), David Bordwell identifies also the other principles of classicism: decorum, proportion, formal harmony, respect for tradition, mimesis, and cool control of the perceiver's response (4).

22. Colin MacCabe, "Realism and the Cinema: Notes on Some Brechtian Theses," *Screen* 15, no. 2 (1974): 8.

23. See, for example, the highly influential "Diderot, Brecht, Eisenstein" by Roland Barthes, in Roland Barthes, *Image—Music—Text* (New York: Hill and Wang, 1977), 69–78.

24. Eisenstein, *Film Form,* 39; emphasis in the original.

25. Friedrich, "On Brecht and Eisenstein," 161.

26. Ibid., 160.

27. The others are "forcing the perspective" through the use of bipolar extremes of lens lengths, reliance on close shots, and wide-ranging camera movements. David Bordwell, *The Way Hollywood Tells It: Story and Style in Modern Movies* (Berkeley: University of California Press, 2006), 121.

28. Theodor W. Adorno, *Aesthetic Theory,* ed. Gretel Adorno and Rolf Tie-

demann, trans. Robert Hullot-Kentor (Minneapolis: University of Minnesota Press, 1997), 155–56. It should be noted that Brecht, unlike Eisenstein, repeatedly expresses wariness of the potential shock-effect of montage. In *The Messingkauf Dialogues* (1939–51), for example, he objects to the Surrealists' use of shock "for entertainment's sake," or—in the phrase of Seong-Kyun Oh—for not aiming for more than a mere destruction of the mundanely familiar. Bertolt Brecht, *The Messingkauf Dialogues,* trans. John Willet (London: Methuen, 1978), 78; Seong-Kyun Oh, *Die materialistisch-dialektische Fundierung des epischen Theaters Brechts als eines zweidimensionalen theatralischen Kommunikationssystems* (Frankfurt am Main: Peter Lang, 1998), 180. Brecht's commentary on the Theatre of the Absurd applies here, too: "Die '*Verfremdung*' des absurden Theaters bleibt bei der '*Entfremdung*' stehen: 'verstehen—nicht verstehen (als Entfremdung)' [alienation, in the Marxist sense of the term]": "the '*Verfremdung* of the absurdist theatre remains at the '*Entfremdung*': 'understanding—not understanding' (as alienation)." Brecht, qtd. in Jan Knopf, *Brecht-Handbuch: Theater* (Stuttgart: J. B. Metzlersche Verlagsbuchhandlung, 1980), 401. Significantly, Brecht planned a rewrite of *Waiting for Godot,* in which the protagonists would be depicted in terms of their class positions: Pozzo would receive an aristocratic "von" and be described as a landowner, Lucky would be "a donkey or a policeman," Estragon a "prole," and Vladimir an "intellectual." Knopf, *Brecht-Handbuch: Theater,* 371.

29. Martin Walsh, *The Brechtian Aspect of Radical Cinema* (London: BFI, 1981), 75.

30. Ibid., 65.

31. Ibid., 61.

32. The association of moving through space and agency, or at least of the mentioned activity and the young man, is further suggested by the scene where the otherwise taciturn character tells the banker an anecdote of Caesar's being captured by the pirates as he walks alongside him.

33. The parallelism between the viewer and the young man is promoted by the film's other instances of self-referentiality. Besides the use of a reformulated shot-countershot syntax, perhaps the most conspicuous of these is black leader, employed to break one of the banker's monologues.

34. Barton Byg, *Landscapes of Resistance: The German Films of Danièle Huillet and Jean-Marie Straub* (Berkeley: University of California Press, 1995), 156.

35. George Lellis, *Bertolt Brecht, Cahiers du cinéma and Contemporary Film Theory* (Ann Arbor, MI: UMI Research Press, 1982), 132.

36. Ibid., 130.

37. Ibid., 132.

38. For more on the question of authorship over Brecht's adaptation of the Sophoclean tragedy, see Robert Savage, "The Precedence of Citation: On Brecht's *The Antigone of Sophocles,*" *Colloquy: Text Theory Critique* 11 (May 2006): 99–126.

39. Bertolt Brecht, *Sophocles' Antigone,* trans. Judith Malina (New York: Applause Theatre Book Publishers, 1990), 20.

40. Ibid., 56.

41. Byg, *Landscapes of Resistance,* 226.

42. Peter Handke, "Antigone," in *Die Früchte des Zorns und der Zärtlichkeit* (Vienna: Viennale, 2004), 118.

43. The prologue features two nameless sisters who find out that their brother has been hanged for deserting the army. As they are preparing to cut the brother's body from the rope, an officer appears. After the sisters' denial that they know each other, the officer asks, "Then what is she doing with the knife?" Brecht, *Sophocles' Antigone,* 14. The prologue ends with the uncertainty of the second sister's next act. "Would she now," asks the first sister, "under the penalty of death / try to free her brother?" By substituting a closure to the scene with the first sister's words ("If only he had not died"), Brecht diverts the focus from the narrative to the question of heroism—both of the second sister and of the heroine of the play proper.

44. Giavarini, qtd. in Byg, *Landscapes of Resistance,* 223.

45. Brecht, *Sophocles' Antigone,* 32.

46. For an interesting (if questionable in its conclusions) discussion of Peter Watkins's relationship to Brecht, see Terry Lajtha's "Brechtian Devices in Non-Brechtian Cinema" *Literature/Film Quarterly* 9, no. 1 (1981): 9–14. For an extensive recent investigation of von Trier's relationship to Brecht, see Anneliese Penzendorfer's *Lars von Triers DOGVILLE: Ein Fusion Film vs. Brechts episches Theater* (VDM Verlag, 2010).

Theatre and Film in Evolutionary Perspective

Bruce McConachie

I

THE ATTITUDES OF American theatre artists and scholars toward film have ranged from disdain and paranoia to curiosity and collaboration during the last 110 years. In the first decade of the last century, when the movies emerged as a viable amusement, theatre artists dismissed film as cheap thrills for immigrants and workers. Only a decade later, after pioneers like D. W. Griffith had demonstrated film's artistic worth and middle-class Americans began flocking to the new movie houses, theatre artists and showbiz moguls wondered if live entertainment would ever again compete for the money of the masses. The "talkies" and the Depression conclusively settled that discussion, and since then the theatrical argument against film shifted to higher, more theoretical ground. Although he defended the mass appeal of film, Walter Benjamin in the 1930s worried that the flickering illusion of actors on a movie screen could never match the "aura" of live performers appearing before audiences. East Coast authors and playwrights, many of them more in love with the written word than with the power of acting, took up Benjamin's concern and turned it against the Hollywood system, even as they also sought fame and fortune by "selling out" to Tinseltown. Despite the fact that Orson Welles, Elia Kazan, and several other directors had proven that theatre and film had a lot to learn from each other, most theatre scholars from midcentury through the mid-1980s, locked into modernist assumptions about the purity of what they believed to be wholly separable media, simply turned their backs on the movies.

These assumptions led to separate disciplines in the academy, despite the obvious commonalities among all forms of live and mediated dramas. Like many academics, we at the University of Pittsburgh have chopped dramatic entertainment into three separate pieces: the Department of Communication does television and video studies, English has film, and Theatre Arts studies and stages plays. In the 1990s, a few scholars (such as Peggy Phelan) continued to pile bricks on these disciplinary walls, while others (like Phil Auslander) questioned the very "liveness" that seemed to distinguish theatre from film and TV. At the same time, several playwrights, including Tony Kushner, were adapting filmic content and techniques for the stage, while directors and designers were immersing spectators in environments that mixed film-derived media, such as video clips and surround-sound, with embodied performance. The discussions and innovations begun in the final decades of the last century continued into the first decade of this one.

If this quick summary proves anything, it may be that envy and paranoia last longer among academics than artists. Most theatre people settled their differences with the movies many years ago. I think it's time for us to do the same. Rather than dwelling on the past hundred years or so—a mere blink in evolutionary time—I'd like us to step much further back and consider theatre and film through the perspective of those affective and cognitive abilities that enable our species to enjoy both media. Certainly there are differences between theatre and film, but how important are they? Most theorists today suppose that ontological divisions separate these media, but I will disagree. The logic of evolution suggests that there is no need to invent new ontological categories to explain human phenomena that are continuous with all of human development and history. Most of the mental operations that *Homo sapiens* deploys to make sense of live performances are also used to understand filmic ones. As I will discuss, human minds reached their present cognitive capabilities about 50,000 years ago; although evolution continues, our major cognitive operations for experiencing the world—performances included—have not changed since then. While there are important historical differences among live and mediated modes of communication, they share a common evolutionary and cognitive foundation.

For evidence, I will draw primarily on evolutionary and developmental psychology. I recognize that understanding my summaries of this kind of evidence will be difficult for most theatre and performance scholars; despite the relevance of many areas of cognitive science to much of our field, our discipline has been slow to take advantage of the cognitive turn in the humanities. I will do what I can to offer straightforward explanations and examples, but a full elaboration of the scientific background would take a book. Indeed, I have already written a book that covers much of this territory—*Engaging Audiences: A Cognitive Approach to Spectating in the Theatre* (2008)[1]—and I would suggest that those wanting more details about such specifics can get many of them there. I will apply much of this evidence to a major example, the rape scene in the theatrical and filmic versions of *A Streetcar Named Desire.* A comparison of the two versions will allow us to highlight similarities and differences between the two media rather than dwelling on the content, style, or directorial vision of one or the other.

Before taking a ride on Williams's *Streetcar,* though, I want you to consider a simpler performance. Imagine a juggling act in which the performer is handling four sticks of wood and keeping three aloft at any one moment. Now place that juggler in the circle of a campfire 50,000 years ago near his band of cohorts, in a Chinese court performing for the emperor about 1,000 years ago, in an Australian circus ring 120 years ago surrounded by cheering workers and families, and finally on film only 100 years ago, when vaudeville spectators in New York enjoyed the same juggling turn that had entranced similar audiences of *Homo sapiens* for centuries. With this example in mind, the question motivating my talk is a simple one: How can we discuss the experience of this juggling act for the performer and his spectators over the course of these 50,000 years? Were all of them unique, varying according to different social and cultural situations? Were there compelling similarities among all of these performances except the last one, when the shift from live to mediated performance created a different kind of experience? Or were all of these performances pretty much alike, regardless of history or medium?

From among these three possible answers, most theorists would choose number two. The shift from live to mediated performance, they assert, involved an ontological change—a change in kind, not simply a change in degree, that might be reflected in the historical contexts. Walter Benjamin, for example, would have asserted that the performance of the juggler and his spectators changed fundamentally when the act appeared on film and viewers were separated from the "aura" of the performer. Benjamin's "The Work of Art in the Age of Mechanical Reproduction" (1936) is often cited by those who believe that the magic of "presence" can occur only when live performers and spectators share the same space at the same time.[2] Because Benjamin never defined "aura" in scientific terms, however, his assertions about it cannot be tested and validated or falsified. Basing her position on Lacanian assumptions, Peggy Phelan has also argued for an ontological distinction between live and mediated performance in her *Unmarked: The Politics of Performance* (1993). In fact, once performances participate in "the circulation of representations of representations" (as occurs with film), they cease to be performances at all for Phelan.[3] Our juggler, to follow that example, had stopped "performing," in Phelan's sense of the term, when he left the circus ring and moved in front of a camera. While Benjamin sidestepped a scientific discussion of his theory, Phelan drew on the pseudo-science of Lacanian psychoanalysis. As I and others have demonstrated, Freudian and Lacanian ideas are not falsifiable; scientists in psychology no longer use the major tenets of psychoanalysis to frame their theories.[4]

In contrast, analytic philosopher Noel Carrol's ontological distinction between live and filmed performances does rest upon tested cognitive realities. In his "Philosophy and Drama: Performance, Interpretation, and Intentionality," Carrol asserts that live is different from mediated because the intentional actions of live performers are ontologically different from the material motions of images in a cinema. When a play is performed, viewers know that the actors intend to communicate and interact directly with them; when watching a film, they know that no such intentionality is possible from the projected images.[5] Recent neuroscientific work on "mirror neurons" validates the reality and importance of intentionality for performance. Networks of such neurons in the frontal lobe of the brain, evident in many higher mammals as well as humans, respond to intentional motor action initiated by others. If an actor/character on stage in a murder melodrama grabs for a gun, the grabbing motion will be picked up by the mirror networks of those sitting in the auditorium; the spectators' mirror networks will fire in much the same way that they would have if each of them had done the grabbing. Although the experimental work on mirror networks in humans is far from complete, many scientists agree that these groups of neurons are fundamental to human empathy. In order to put yourself in the shoes (and mind) of another person, whether on stage or elsewhere, you must be able to read that person's intentions and emotions. Through mirror network processing of the muscles in another's face and body, plus other cognitive operations, humans are able to pick up significant information about the other's emotions and intentions, information that unconsciously informs empathetic response.[6] Sparked by intentional action, our mirror networks kick in unconsciously hundreds of times a day, both in performance situations and in regular everyday life.

Given mirror networks and their links to empathy, Carrol is correct about the importance of intentionality. But is this enough to validate his position? From his point of view, watching a film is the same as looking at objects in motion. He states, "Since mass-mediatized artworks are types of artworks that rely upon templates to produce token performances, mass-mediatized artworks differ categorically from dramatic performances that rely on intentional states—interpretative acts—in order to be made manifest. . . . For, were *Cats* [the musical] performed by zombies, I do not think we would be comfortable with calling the performance live nor the troupe a living theatre."[7] This is narrowly true with regard to the actors' performances in the moment of their projection. In the movie house only the projectionist exerts any intentionality when it comes to showing filmic images on the screen; the performer's work is already "in the can." Our juggler in the previous example might even be seated in the audience, watching an edited version of his act before the camera, but exerting no intentionality with the audience while the film rolls. Carrol recognizes, of course, that there was a lot of human intentionality that went into the making of the film, but he draws his ontological distinction on the grounds that this past work is not present to the audience when they watch the film. Because film actors and spectators cannot interact with each other in the flesh during a film showing, live is fundamentally different from filmed performance.[8]

This is a well-reasoned position, dependent on a foundational difference between animate subjects and inanimate objects. Allowing for Carrol's animate/inanimate ontology, however, are there cognitive operations that effectively bypass this apparent problem? To get some perspective on this, and to resolve the problem of Carrol's attempt at an ontological distinction between mediated and live, it will be helpful to move to an evolutionary understanding of performance.

II

Where did live performance come from and why? And how is it that *Homo sapiens* has been able to adjust rather easily to so many modes of mediated performance since roughly the turn of the twentieth century? While there is no broad agreement on the answers to these questions, a consensus is emerging among those biologists, evolutionary psychologists, cognitive philosophers, and literary critics who are exploring the species-level origins and ramifications of mammalian play, cognitive flexibility, and artistic expression among humans. In his *On the Origin of Stories: Evolution, Cognition, and Fiction* (2009), Brian Boyd provides an excellent synthesis of much of the current knowledge on these matters.[9] I will primarily follow his path into this thicket, with a few detours along the way to incorporate other relevant research. Although Boyd does not deal specifically with the live versus mediated debates, his insights, garnered from several hundred scientific accounts and theories, set the stage for investigating this problem and Carrol's ontological take on it.

According to Boyd—and many others would agree—our impulse to craft performances and to engage with the performances of others comes from our evolutionary heritage of play. What are the typical attributes of play, as scholars have come to understand them? Because the scientific research on animal play far outweighs the research focused solely on human play, most scholars begin with characteristics that are widely shared among all playing animals, including *Homo sapiens.* According to Robert Fagen, one of the celebrated researchers in the field, "Play occurs in only a small minority of the Earth's million or more species. Animal play is easy to recognize. Specific movement qualities and signal patterns characterize the familiar play behavior of cats, dogs, and human children as well as the play of other animals. Mammals and birds, and perhaps a few fishes and reptiles, are the only kinds of animals known to play."[10] Fagen's categories of animal play include brief repetitive acts by rodents, running and jumping performed singly by some mammals and birds, and the sparring and wrestling of primates and carnivores. Although animals use objects or features of the landscape to play apparent versions of hide-and-seek and follow-the-leader, they cannot invent games or rules for their play.

Nonetheless, these examples point up several continuities between animal play and the play of *Homo sapiens.* Although other playing animals cannot approach the cognitive complexities of *Hamlet* or baseball, they, like us, recognize play as a distinct event with its own "conventions." Among other things, this means that members of the same species understand that a playful exchange need not arouse a fight or flight response. Second, from Fagen's descriptions of these activities and from numerous experiments performed on playing animals, it is clear that these animals, especially the young of the species, will seek out opportunities to play. At some level, these mammals and birds "intend" to play. Rather than simply responding automatically to external stimuli, they will take up play spontaneously. Finally, animals "enjoy" their mutual play. Scientists know this because they have tracked chemical changes associated with joyful emotions in the brains of mammals during and after play. Consequently, play is self-reinforcing. As the foundation of all performance, the activity of play already entails notions of intentionality, enjoyment, and event.

With this kind of evidence in hand, many scientists have concluded that play is an evolutionary adaptation. That is, play is a species-wide behavior in some mammals, birds, and others that functions in ways that ultimately helped and continues to facilitate those species' ability to survive. Boyd summarizes the logic and evidence that lead to this conclusion:

> Play evolved through the advantages of flexibility; the amount of play in a species correlates with its flexibility of action. Behaviors like escape and pursuit, attack and defense, and social give-and-take can make life-or-death differences. Creatures with more motivation to practice such behaviors in situations of low urgency can fare better at moments of high urgency. Animals that play repeatedly and exuberantly refine skills, extend repertoires, and sharpen sensitivities. Play therefore has evolved to be highly self-rewarding. Because it is compulsive, animals engage in it again and again, incrementally altering muscle tone and neural wiring, strengthening and increasing speed in synaptic pathways, improving their capacity and performance.[11]

What has worked evolutionarily for rats, dogs, and elephants has also worked for us. It is likely that our hominid ancestors had been playing for over six million years, the estimated time when our eventual species parted ways genetically from our near relations, the proto-chimpanzees.

Since then, judging from the increasing size of hominid skulls and other clues, our ancestors survived as much by their wits and sociality as by their physical acumen and reproductive ability. According to Boyd, playing allowed proto-humans to flourish because it increased their cognitive flexibility, especially their ability to recognize, repeat, and refine patterns. Boyd defines pattern broadly as any discernible arrangement of order or form; humans normally see patterns in a face, the night sky, and a narrative story. He particularly emphasizes the cognitive patterns—patterns of sound, design, words, and/or action—embedded in artistic creation and reception. Such patterns constitute his view of art as "a kind of cognitive *play,* the set of activities designed to engage human *attention* through their own appeal to our preference for inferentially rich and therefore *patterned* information."[12] Like the other arts, performances helped evolving hominids to pattern their lives, coordinating curiosity, memory, attention, and empathy in socially engaged and open-ended ways. Boyd is clear that "even if it diverts energy away from immediate survival or reproductive needs, [art] can improve cooperation within a group enough for the group to compete successfully against others with less inclination to art." He adds, "We should think in the first place not of art galleries or concert halls . . . , but of chants, drums, dance, body-markings, costumes, banners and the like."[13] The performances of our ancestors probably increased the survivability of our species.

Given its links to survival, performance and the other arts probably preceded religious rituals in our evolutionary past. There is good evidence to reverse the assumption of many theorists that art grew out of religion. Boyd notes that while the earliest sketchy evidence for religious practice dates from 90,000 years ago, ocher has been used for body decoration for at least 120,000 years and probably much longer. Hominids already habituated to dancing and singing for each other likely presumed that their gods would perceive and enjoy their performances in the same ways. Since religious belief plus artistic production amplifies social cohesion, those early bands that worshipped and performed together also thrived together.

Several anthropologists attuned to the new insights of cognitive science have taken a fresh look at the likely evolutionary origins of religion. Stewart Guthrie, Jonathan Lanman, Justin Barrett, and Harvey Whitehouse emphasize the importance of the Hypersensitive Agency Detective Device (HADD) in the minds of hominids and later *Homo sapiens* as a primary reason for our species' creation and worship of gods.[14] Many psychological experiments have demonstrated that people often claim that they have detected animate agency in images, natural events, and accidents where none really exists. People believe they can see the face of a deity in the embers of a fire, for example, or are able to perceive the workings of the gods in a thunderstorm. In these instances, they have projected their own notion of agency into a situation they cannot explain to enable them to understand it as the will of some almighty power.

Evolution primed our species to be hypersensitive about invisible agents that might do them harm. Better to interpret that rustling behind the bush as a lurking tiger about to pounce than to ignore the signs of possible agency! On those few occasions when such interpretations were correct, the hunter-gatherer might survive. Furthermore, the cost of false positives in such situations was relatively trivial. Guthrie, Lanman, Barrett, and Whitehouse presume that a belief in unseen higher powers often operated in the same ways in our past and continues to shape religious belief today. Better to believe, like the rest of the tribe, that the gods might curse your hunting or blight your crops than to risk offending unseen but always lurking animate powers. Better still to try to propitiate such deities, even if the rituals that your tribe formulated were seldom effective. HADD, initially an evolutionary adaptation that sensitized our ancestors to the possibility of dangerous agency, led to the secondary cognitive effect of helping them to invent and perpetuate religion.

This is not to say that HADD is the only cognitive mechanism behind religious belief and ritual. There is no single module in our brains that facilitates religion. Like most complex, social-psychological systems, including performance, religion depends upon a number of neurological as well as cultural operations to flourish. This essay is not the place to elaborate all of the mental systems and cultural institutions that had to be in place before *Homo sapiens* could create, refine, and enjoy performances. Nonetheless, a summary of these evolutionary developments will be helpful to remind ourselves that live performance, though apparently quite simple when compared to its mediated cousins, is actually an amazingly complex and flexible phenomenon in contrast to the play activities of other higher mammals. I will draw on my own and others' scholarship to summarize the major cognitive operations that help to constitute performance.

Substantial evidence about the enlargement of the frontal lobes in the human brain and physical developments that facilitated articulate speech suggests that modern *Homo sapiens* stepped onto the evolutionary stage roughly 50,000 years ago. By then, we had evolved much better memories than other animals, for example. Dolphins performing at SeaWorld can remember instructions, but their minds are restricted primarily to episodic memory (which allows for the recollection of specific events) rather than the combination of episodic and semantic memory (which facilitates the recall of several types of patterns, including language) in humans. Likewise, many higher animals have mirror networks that grant them a degree of empathy, but the human ability to understand the beliefs, desires, and intentions of others in our species is unsurpassed in the animal kingdom.[15] Although we share the same primary emotions with many higher mammals, we, unlike them, can gain consciousness of our emotions and recognize them as feelings.

Other attributes of *Homo sapiens* that facilitate performance are further removed from our evolutionary past. Our pattern-recognition systems allow us to frame certain events as "performances" and to move in and out of those frames instantaneously. Consequently, along with our ancestors 50,000 years ago, we can engage with a dramatic fiction in a performance space in one moment and wonder what is wrong with a spectator who is coughing near us in the next. Well before Brecht came along to tell us to do so, we were able to multitask at performances, easily jumping among frames of fiction, direct address, and musical modes of performance. Facilitating such multitasking at performances is conceptual blending, the cognitive operation identified by Gilles Fauconnier and Mark Turner, that enables us to merge actors and characters together, a cognitive integration necessary for spectators as well as performers.[16] Blending creates the doubleness of all performance, the knowledge that the juggler is both himself and a carefully crafted role that he is playing. While not all performances then or now involve narrative, many employ a sequence of actions that challenges spectators to put together patterns of causal relationships that tell a story. Finally, there is vocal language, a late evolutionary addition that certainly enabled the creation and rehearsal of many kinds of performances as well as their enactment and reception 50,000 years ago. The structure of language does not provide the template for performance, as some structuralist and poststructuralist theorists have presumed; the evolutionary fundamentals of performance belong to play. But language did enhance and extend role-playing and narrative possibilities.

This summary of the major cognitive advances in place around 50,000 years ago that enabled our ancestors' performances gives us a kind of baseline for all subsequent modes of performing. Obviously, we did not suddenly develop major new mental abilities in the twentieth century to facilitate our understanding of film; evolution never works that fast. So one question that this summary poses is how did we use our evolved cognitive operations to accommodate the performance media that have proliferated since the twentieth century. We have already seen that HADD, initially a direct aid in survival, had the secondary effect of sparking religious belief and ritual. We can assume that our mental adjustments to the new media may also have drawn on cognitive operations not usually deployed for live performance to enable us to produce and understand filmed performances. But what were they? And, finally, what are the ontological ramifications, if any, of this shift from mostly live to predominantly mediated performances in the twentieth century?

III

As it turns out, the answer to the last question opens up the possibility of addressing the previous ones. Cognitive philosopher Mark Johnson's understanding of the logic of continuity in naturalistic theory is the key to the ontological problem. Johnson borrows continuity theory from John Dewey, who based its assumptions on Darwinian evolution. Since all life evolved from previously living things, there can be no ontological breaks in animal and human history, noted Dewey. As Johnson elaborates,

> The principle of continuity entails that any explanation of the nature and workings of mind, even the most abstract conceptualization and reasoning, must have its roots in the embodied capacities of the organism for perception, feeling, object manipulation, and bodily movement. The continuity hypothesis, however, does not entail that there are no demarcations, differentiations, or distinctions within experience. Of course there are demarcations, and they are very real and important! The continuity hypothesis insists only that wherever and whenever we find actual working distinctions, they are explicable against the background of continuous processes. Furthermore, social and cultural forces are required to develop our cognitive capacities to their full potential, including language and symbolic

> reasoning. Infants do not speak or discover mathematical proofs at birth. Dewey's continuity thesis thus requires both evolutionary and developmental explanations.[17]

For Johnson, evolutionary continuity is an important key to avoiding unnecessary ontological dualisms. Following continuity theory, we can expect that new ideas and practices emerged out of previous ones; differences of degree are much more likely than differences of kind. In terms of the live and mediated debate, it is clear that live performances emerged from our evolutionary past as playful mammals and that post-1900 mediated performances developed out of live ones. Consequently, we should expect no ontological breaks in this continuous process.

Assuming this is so, I should be able to explain the cognitive basis of all mediated performances with most of the same cognitive tools that I have used to account for live performance. And, if I must introduce a new cognitive operation not necessary for live performance, it must be an ability that was present in the minds of *Homo sapiens* 50,000 years ago. As it happens, this is not difficult to do. Justin Barrett, writing about the Hypersensitive Agency Detection Device in our heads, notes that HADD not only induces a belief in deities, but also "makes us nonreflectively believe . . . that light patterns on a television screen are people or animals with beliefs and desires."[18] The cognitive operation is the same for film as for TV: because viewers see a phenomenon that appears to possess some independent agency and looks to be human, they project their notion of human intentionality onto it. In short, HADD made it easy for viewers to believe in the sights, and later the sounds, of early-twentieth-century performers on film.

Of course viewers need not project their notions of human intentionality onto screen images. If they wish, they can, like Noel Carrol, refuse to credit such mechanical reproductions with real intentions. But to hold to this position contradicts how audiences actually watch films and, arguably, the way they were meant to be enjoyed. Evolution fashioned us to project intentionality onto all kinds of objects and images; HADD is a part of who we are as a species. Operating within the constraints and possibilities of such folk psychology may not be ontologically correct, from some philosophical points of view, but it is certainly natural.

IV

Most critics and historians have emphasized the major differences between the 1947 Broadway production of Tennessee Williams's *A Streetcar Named Desire* and the film, released in 1951. Although Williams did most of the script adaptation and Kazan and much of the Broadway cast remained, the Hollywood producers hired Vivian Leigh to replace Jessica Tandy as Blanche and pressured Williams and Kazan to accommodate censorship from the industry's board and the Catholic Legion of Decency. Despite these differences and problems, I will emphasize the many commonalities in the script and the directorial vision between the stage and film versions so that we can focus on the two media, through an examination of the climactic rape scene.

I will briefly discuss Williams and Kazan's work on the film before moving to comparisons between the live and mediated versions of *Streetcar.* Hollywood hired an adapter to work with Williams, but the evidence makes it clear that Tennessee did nearly all of the revisions himself. His script for Warner Brothers cuts the published drama that emerged from the Broadway production, of course, but the story and character relationships remain nearly the same. In his revision, Williams got around the censors by inserting circumlocutions about Blanche's past and removing the few suggestions that she might be partly to blame for her present sexualized relationship with Stanley. Regarding the rape scene itself, Williams wanted it to be understood as "the ravishment of the tender, the sensitive, the delicate, by the savage and brutal forces of modern society."[19] I expect that most viewers today and in 1951 would agree that the scene largely affirms Williams's hopes for it. Part of its emotional effectiveness is the climactic moment of the beer bottle smashing into the oval mirror, a metaphor for the rape itself, which Kazan carefully sets up through previous shots. The censors would not allow Kazan to suggest the brutality of Brando/Stanley's rape by depicting the two of them in bed, so Kazan had to find an indirect means of telling the story. Film critic Linda Costanzo Cahir nicely affirms the ironic victory of Williams and Kazan over Hollywood's conventionality in the thesis for her short article, entitled "The Artful Rerouting of *A Streetcar Named Desire*": "The success of the film, oddly, is due in part to the way in which Kazan and Williams turned the tables and made potentially destructive constraints work constructively in the movie."[20]

Because the film mostly captures what we might generally call Williams's intentions for his play, we can use its productions on Broadway and in Hollywood to focus on the live versus mediated debate. We can begin by noting two obvious but frequently overlooked differences between the stage and the film versions. Were you watching the film in a typical movie theatre in 1951, the apparent sizes of Brando and Leigh on the screen would have been huge compared to the sizes of the flesh-and-blood Brando and Tandy on the stage in 1947, even if you happened to be sitting in the front row. Size matters for humans. Because big objects and animals were more likely to present threats to our survival, we evolved to pay attention to size.[21] Kazan chose medium and close-up shots for most of the rape scene, giving Leigh/Blanche several close-ups to heighten her sympathetic appeal. Again, for reasons of survival, our hominid ancestors were more likely to track moving rather than still agents.[22] As a stage director, Kazan was notorious for keeping his actors in motion, but film, of course—because of the addition of a moving camera to the actors' blocking—offered him more opportunities. The end of the rape scene takes place in a metaphorical jungle, with a moving predator, initially shot from behind to increase his size, stalking and finally cornering his prey. The combination of size and movement in the filmed rape scene, capped by Leigh/Blanche's frantic wrestling and the shattered mirror at the end, produces both fluid and startling effects.

I want to focus on the emotions produced in spectators by the rape scene because our emotions evolved to orient us in fundamental ways to the environment and to other living things. Without emotions to protect and inform our adaptability, sociality, and even our morality, our species would have been dead meat long ago. Although scientists vary in their definitions and understandings of emotion, the cognitive turn in the humanities now facilitates informed discussions about the role of the emotions in shaping spectator response and meaning. In particular, I will rely on Carl Plantinga's broad synthesis of phenomenology and scientific evidence in his 2009 book, *Moving Viewers: American Film and the Spectator's Experience.* Following a rigorous discussion of the science involved, Plantinga introduces a typology of spectator responses that produce emotions. These cognitive operations include direct responses, which take narrative content as their object, local responses of brief duration, usually inspired by a cinematic effect, and sympathetic or antipathetic responses, emotions generated by specific actors/characters. Each of these types of response may evoke various emotions, ranging from fear and disgust to curiosity and joy. Using Plantinga as our guide, we might say that the rape scene probably evoked suspense and some surprise directly through the narrative and startled excitement at the local effect of the beer bottle smashing into the mirror. Regarding spectator response to the actors/characters, Brando/Stanley's actions probably produced some happiness initially, but fear and disdain in most viewers after he decided to "interfere with" Blanche. In contrast, Leigh/Blanche likely evoked compassion early in the scene, some admiration when she opposed Stanley in the middle of it, and mostly pity and fear at the end. Plantinga does not assume that all spectators will respond in the same ways; nor do I. But he is persuasive in arguing that popular films must create a clear and compelling rhetoric of emotions in order to succeed with most spectators. I agree. And, judging from *Streetcar*'s award-winning popularity in 1951 and '52, most viewers, while disturbed or even shocked by what they saw, were not confused or put off by what Plantinga would call the emotional rhetoric of the film.[23]

This was not the case in 1947 and '48, when the play was produced on Broadway. Several of the New York critics found Brando's Stanley to be a likeable, if passionate, fellow and condemned Tandy's Blanche as a neurotic nymphomaniac. Reviewer William Hawkins spoke for several others in remarking on Blanche's "unrelenting hopelessness" and her "desperate falseness." Consequently, he concluded, "[Tandy] makes her pathos repellent rather than sympathetic."[24] No less an authority than Marlon Brando agreed. In his 1994 autobiography, he concluded that he and Tandy were both miscast. "She was too shrill to elicit the sympathy . . . the woman deserved. This threw the play out of balance because the audience was not able to recognize the potential of her character, and as a result my character got a more sympathetic reaction than Tennessee intended."[25] Perhaps confused by or accepting of the rape itself, the reviewers had little to say about it. When they did not ignore it, they couched their comments in euphemism and evasion; none of them expressed sympathy for Tandy/Blanche at the climactic end of that scene. Unlike the film, there seems to have been no symbolically charged moment on the stage similar to the beer bottle smashing into the mirror.

Clearly, the lack of a heightened local response and the shift in the balance of sympathy and antipathy between Blanche and Stanley, to adopt Plantinga's terminology, generated different emotions in the theatregoing audience of 1947 than among filmgoers in 1951. Evidently, fewer theatregoers were surprised by the rape, some were willing to blame Tandy/Blanche for Brando/Stanley's aggression, and Tandy did not evoke as much compassion and pity for her Blanche as did Leigh in the film. Again, this is not to say that all theatregoers had the same response and that all film viewers reacted very differently a few years later. But, in general, it appears that the film succeeded better than the stage performance in fulfilling Williams's goal of presenting the ravishment of a sensitive and delicate Blanche by the brutal force of Stanley. As I have noted, substituting Leigh for Tandy in the key role of Blanche certainly made a difference in the balance of sympathies. It may be, too, that Kazan realized that he had to center more of the film on Leigh's Blanche than on the shared emphasis between Stanley and Blanche that he had fostered for the stage version. Certainly the Hollywood moguls wanted to heighten the importance of their star and spectators, trained by over twenty years of film viewing since the talkies, would have looked to Vivian Leigh and her role to orient their response to *Streetcar*. For film viewers who had seen recent revivals of *Gone with the Wind,* of course, Leigh's Blanche was easily understood as a darker version of the headstrong Southern belle trying to adapt to more modern and more difficult circumstances.

But were there factors unique to the experience of live or mediated viewing that also made a difference in the general reception of both *Streetcars*? Although Kazan added the bottle-mirror crash to the film, similar effects are certainly possible on the stage. We have all been riveted by such moments in live performances, and the sudden change in focus that they command from spectators is not unlike a camera close-up. Instead, I'd suggest that we look at the dynamics of empathy and spatiality in live and mediated performance. Evolution trained our species to learn to read the emotions and intentions of other people in live, three-dimensional environments. Film can give us close-ups of faces, of course, where emotions and intentions are often readily legible, but it does not usually register continuous interpersonal and environmental spatial relations. As we know, the early movies often put an entire staged scene on celluloid, but these long shots were not very successful. The human eye and mind do not perceive what we might call a full proscenium view on film with the same interest and engagement that occurs when we pay attention to live action on a conventional proscenium stage.

I suspect that this is because evolution linked our mirror neurons and our other empathetic operations to our ability to estimate what scientist J. J. Gibson has termed the "affordances" that guide our interactions and movements with others and the environment. Gibson began using this term in the 1960s to describe how humans evaluate their own and others' movement possibilities within a given place, and cognitive psychologists have continued to find his insights compelling.[26] Place is important for survival; we all know "instinctively" that narrow canyons are more dangerous than grasslands with trees. As drivers, we have to fight the tendency to tense up when we drive through tunnels or enter tightly enclosed spaces. As we know from production work in film, however, place is fungible on a movie set and the illusion of actual entrapment may be sacrificed to emphasize character interaction. Furniture and scenery can be moved and relit to accommodate a specific shot without disturbing continuity and believability for the viewer. Kazan took advantage of this possibility on the Hollywood set for *Streetcar;* furniture disappears, rooms expand and contract, and each shot gets its own particular lighting. Such flexibility is impossible in the theatre, of course, especially within the duration of a single scene. Even when minimal sets are used and quickly changed, spectators at a play always know the "affordances" that the actors are working within. Their empathetic response will be keyed as much to the whole-body movements of the actors' muscles in that stage environment as to their eye and facial muscles in their interpersonal relationships. Spectator empathy with filmed actors/characters in an environment is never totally eliminated, of course, especially for those films that are shot on location. But it is usually diminished, in part so that our response to the interpersonal relationships among the actors/characters can be heightened. Where spectators at a film may temporarily forget the affordances for movement allowed to actors/characters, audiences in a theatre never do.

The action of *Streetcar*, on film or on stage, requires a trapped Blanche for the rape scene. For the film, Kazan carefully shot Brando/Stanley closing the apartment door and then closing in on Blanche to corner her in the back bedroom. But until the moment when Stanley blocks Blanche's path to the outdoors, it seems as though she might have been able to escape into the New Orleans night. In contrast, the spatial relations of the rape scene on Jo Mielziner's Broadway set in 1947 carried meanings that were not possible in the film. On stage, Blanche is discovered in the back bedroom at the top of the scene, a room that she has attempted to remake as a place of fantasy, nostalgia, and hope. By this point in the action, however, Williams has ensured that spectators will have a more complex understanding of this space; it may be a place for Blanche's fantasies, but it is also the scene of Stella and Stanley's lovemaking and, just as importantly, the room affords only one way out, through the real world of the kitchen area and into the street. In other words, any Blanche—not just Tandy's—who begins the scene in the back bedroom of a Mielziner-like set for *Streetcar* has already partly trapped herself. The sheer weight and affordances of the small apartment, plus the meanings the bedroom has already accrued, would create an atmosphere of doom as soon as Stanley discovers her in that bedroom. To put this another way, the rape scene on the Broadway stage in 1947 was not just about character relationships, although Tandy/Blanche and Brando/Stanley's mutual attraction and disdain must certainly have played an important part in shaping spectator response. The scene was also about the physical affordances that trapped a lost belle into a dead-end bedroom controlled by an urban brute. On stage, Stanley's material world afforded no room for Blanche's softness and sensitivity.

Because material place always registers with spectators on stage but may be elided on film, spatial affordances often play a more important role in shaping spectator empathy in the theatre than at the movies. I realize that this insight is counterintuitive; we usually think of films in contrast to stage plays as opening out our spatial imaginations. Of course the movies can incorporate more scenic vistas, but scenery alone does not spark our mirror neurons. Our neural networks are keyed to bodies interacting intentionally in a specific place, and this interaction is a continuously unfolding process in the theatre, whether within a realistic set or on a bare stage. Consequently, spatial affordances often affect the perceived balance of sympathy and antipathy among actors/characters in the playhouse. The continuous presence throughout the performance of Mielziner's set and Tandy/Blanche's presence within it at the top of the rape scene probably contributed to spectators' anticipation that something dreadful would happen to this trapped protagonist. All other factors being equal, a filmed version of *Streetcar* will probably encourage audiences to see a Blanche who has more freedom of action than a Blanche on stage. And, because she cannot act on that freedom in the rape scene, this will likely lead spectators to accord more sympathy and pity to a Blanche on film than will occur in the theatre. Ironically, perhaps, film was better suited than the theatre for realizing Williams's hopes and intentions for the climactic scene of his play.

Notes

1. Bruce McConachie, *Engaging Audiences: A Cognitive Approach to Spectating in the Theatre* (New York: Palgrave Macmillan, 2008).

2. Walter Benjamin, "The Work of Art in the Age of Mechanical Reproduction (1936)," in *Video Culture: A Critical Investigation,* ed. John Hanhardt (Layton, UT: Peregrine Smith Books, 1986), 27–52.

3. Peggy Phelan, *Unmarked: The Politics of Performance* (London: Routledge, 1993), 146.

4. See Bruce McConachie, "Cognitive Studies and Epistemic Competence in Cultural History: Moving beyond Freud and Lacan," in *Performance and Cognition: Theatre Studies and the Cognitive Turn,* ed. Bruce McConachie and F. Elizabeth Hart (London: Routledge, 2006), 52–75, for my own and others' understanding of Lacan's scientific shortcomings.

Other theorists in the live versus mediated debates take an ontological position without realizing they are doing so. Philip Auslander assumes he is urging a historical point of view, but he backs into an ontology also at odds with the demands of falsifiability. He bases his key arguments on Baudrillard, whose poststructuralism cannot be reconciled with the embodied realism implicit in much cognitive science. Philip Auslander, *Liveness: Performance in a Mediatized Culture,* 2nd ed. (London: Routledge, 2008). For a discussion of embodiment and poststructuralism, see George Lakoff and Mark Johnson, *Philosophy in the Flesh: The Embodied Mind and Its Challenge to Western Thought* (New York: Basic Books, 1999), 463–67.

5. Noel Carrol, "Philosophy and Drama: Performance, Interpretation, and Intentionality," in *Staging Philosophy: Intersections of Theater, Performance, and Philosophy,* ed. David Krasner and David Z. Saltz (Ann Arbor: University of

Michigan Press, 2006), 104–21. Initially persuaded by Carrol's position, I endorsed it in *Engaging Audiences*, 57–58. I have since changed my mind.

6. On empathy, see Evan Thompson, *Mind in Life: Biology, Phenomenology, and the Sciences of Mind* (Cambridge, MA: Belknap Press, 2007), 382–411.

7. Carrol, "Philosophy and Drama," 115.

8. Carrol, "Philosophy and Drama," 119.

9. Brian Boyd, *On the Origin of Stories: Evolution, Cognition, and Fiction* (Cambridge, MA: Belknap Press, 2009), 80–125. Despite its recent publication, Boyd's book has already been widely and very favorably reviewed by leading literary critics, biologists, and others. See the Website of Harvard University Press for reviews and excerpts from the book: http://www.hup.harvard.edu/catalog/php?recid=30825.

10. Robert Fagen, "Animal Play, Games of Angels: Biology and Brain," in *The Future of Play Theory*, ed. A. D. Pellegrini (Albany: State University of New York Press, 1995), 24.

11. Boyd, *On the Origin of Stories*, 14.

12. Ibid., 85; emphasis in original.

13. Ibid., 106.

14. See Stewart Elliott Guthrie, "Anthropology and Anthropomorphism in Religion"; Jonathan A. Lanman, "How 'Natives' Don't Think: The Apotheosis of Overinterpretation"; Justin L. Barrett, "Gods"; and Harvey Whitehouse, "Towards an Integration of Ethnography, History, and the Cognitive Science of Religion," in *Religion, Anthropology, and Cognitive Science*, ed. Harvey Whitehouse and James Laidlaw (Durham, NC: Carolina Academic Press, 2007), 37–62, 105–32, 179–207, 247–80.

15. In addition to Boyd, *On the Origin of Stories*, see Merlin Donald, *A Mind So Rare: The Evolution of Human Consciousness* (New York: W. W. Norton, 2001), 1–300.

16. Gilles Fauconnier and Mark Turner, *The Way We Think: Conceptual Blending and the Mind's Hidden Complexities* (New York: Basic Books, 2002), 1–59, 249–69. See also my elaboration of blending for spectatorship in *Engaging Audiences*, 47–55.

17. Mark Johnson, *The Meaning of the Body: Aesthetics of Human Understanding* (Chicago: University of Chicago Press, 2007), 122–23.

18. Barrett, "Gods," 189.

19. Qtd. in Linda Costanzo Cahir, "The Artful Rerouting of *A Streetcar Named Desire*," *Literature/Film Quarterly* 22, no. 2(April 1994): 75.

20. Ibid., 72.

21. Byron Reeves and Clifford Nass, *The Media Equation: How People Treat Computers, Television, and New Media Like Real People and Places* (New York: Cambridge University Press, 1996).

22. B. Reeves, E. Thorson, M. L. Rothschild, D. McDonald, R. Goldstein, and J. Hirsch, "Attention to Television: Intrastimulus Effects of Movement and Scene Changes on Alpha Variation over Time," *International Journal of Neuroscience* 27 (1985): 241–55.

23. See Carl Plantinga, *Moving Viewers: American Film and the Spectator's Experience* (Berkeley: University of California Press, 2009), 198–230.

24. William Hawkins, "Streetcar a Fine Play of Clashing Emotions," *(New York World Telegram), New York Theatre Critics Reviews,* vol. 8, 1947, 251. I have discussed the 1947 reception of *Streetcar* in *American Theater in the Culture of the Cold War: Producing and Contesting Containment, 1947–1962* (Iowa City: University of Iowa Press, 2003), 86–100.

25. Qtd. in McConachie, *American Theater in the Culture of the Cold War,* 97.

26. See my discussion of Gibson's ideas in McConachie, *Engaging Audiences,* 131–33.

Contributors

Becky Becker teaches theatre history, script analysis, and playwriting and heads the BA program in theatre at Columbus State University in Columbus, Georgia. Her directing credits include *The Conduct of Life, Once on This Island, A Midsummer Night's Dream, The Laramie Project, Machinal,* and *Cloud Nine*. She has also conceived and directed several oral history performances: *Westville: Collected Lives,* describing the founding of a historic 1850s village in Georgia, and *Bibb City: Collected Lives from a Mill Town,* chronicling mill life on the Chattahoochee River. She developed an interest in Nigeria after interviewing Nigeria-born playwright Tess Onwueme, visiting Nigeria on a faculty development seminar in 2008, and, most recently, helping to plan a conference on Onwueme's work in 2009. Her published work may be found in *American Drama, Theatre Journal,* and *Feminist Teacher.*

Steve Earnest is an associate professor of theatre at Coastal Carolina University. In addition to practical work as a director and actor, his continued research examines international theatre training programs in Germany and Iceland. He holds a PhD in theatre from the University of Colorado, Boulder, and an MFA in musical theatre from the University of Miami.

Anthony Hostetter's first book, *Max Reinhardt's Grosses Schauspielhaus: Its Artistic Goals, Planning, and Operation, 1910–1933,* was published in 2003. He won the 2001 Herbert D. Greggs Award for Outstanding Writing in Theatre Design and Technology for his peer-reviewed article "A Disaster of Cosmic Proportions? Revisiting Max Reinhardt's Grosses

Schauspielhaus." He has had reviews published by *Theatre Journal* and *Communications from the International Brecht Society* in 2008 and 2009. His "An Interview with John Clancy, Playwright and Director," was published in *Communications from the International Brecht Society*, in the spring of 2009.

Elisabeth Hostetter is an associate professor of theatre and dance at Rowan University in Glassboro, New Jersey. In 2005, Edwin Mellen Press published her first book, *The Berlin State Theater under the Nazi Regime.* She and her husband, Dr. Anthony Hostetter, are cofounders of the In Other Words Project that helps promote recent translations of politically relevant work from other countries. Her interest in German theatre earned her a National Endowment for the Humanities Award to study Bertolt Brecht in Berlin. She received her PhD in theatre history from the University of Missouri, her MA from the University of Texas at Austin, and her BFA from Virginia Commonwealth University.

Nenad Jovanovic (BFA, MFA) has written and directed film and theatre, as well as authored several books of poetry and fiction in the Serbo-Croat language. He is a doctoral candidate in the Graduate Centre for Study of Drama at the University of Toronto. His article "Brook, Lear, and the Modified Verfremdung" is forthcoming in *Literature/Film Quarterly.*

Bruce McConachie is chair of Theatre Arts at the University of Pittsburgh and has written widely on U.S. theatre history, historiography, and cognitive science and performance. His recent books include *Performance and Cognition* (coedited with F. Elizabeth Hart, 2006) and *Engaging Audiences: A Cognitive Approach to Spectating in the Theatre* (2008). He is also the coeditor of the Cognitive Studies in Literature and Performance series for Palgrave Macmillan.

Lawrence D. Smith is a doctoral candidate in theatre history and cinema studies at the University of Illinois Urbana-Champaign. His research concerns the use and representation of traditional performance practices (theatre, dance, circus, variety, community ritual, etc.) in European auteur cinema. He received a Swedish Institute Fellowship for research at the Ingmar Bergman Foundation Archives, was a Research Group member in Cognitive Studies in Theatre and Performance at ASTR (2009), and has presented papers at the Symposium on Theatre and Cognitive Studies, University of Pittsburgh (2009), and at the Midwest Regional Meeting of the American Conference for Irish Studies (2008).

His article "Readymades, Rejects and the Ready-to-Hand: Found Objects in the Films of Aki Kaurismäki" is in the current edition of the *Scandinavian-Canadian Studies Journal.*

Erin Bone Steele is in the PhD program at the University of Maryland, where her focus is nineteenth-century true-crime melodrama. She has presented work at the Mid-American Theatre Conference, at the Southeastern Theatre Conference Theatre History Symposium, and at the Attending to Early Modern Women symposium. Her book chapter "Alice Arden and Her Accomplices: Husband-Murder on the Early Modern Stage," coauthored with Marisha Caswell, is forthcoming in the anthology *Women Who Murder* from Edwin Mellen Press. Erin also works teaching youth theatre workshops, dramaturging, and directing.

Nathan Stith is a theatre graduate student at the University of Colorado at Boulder. Before returning to the world of academic theatre, Nathan spent fifteen years in New York City working as an actor, including performances in national tours of *Jesus Christ Superstar* and *Romeo and Juliet,* an appearance at the New York Metropolitan Opera with Plácido Domingo, and in numerous productions off-Broadway and regionally throughout the country. Nathan recently worked as a dramaturg for the Colorado Shakespeare Festival's 2010 season.

Leslie A. Wade, a scholar in contemporary American and British theatre, is the author of *Sam Shepard and the American Theater.* Les served many years as the program head of doctoral studies in the Louisiana State University Department of Theatre. He also codirected the LSU in London program. He is currently a professor and playwright in the Department of Drama at the University of Arkansas.